TWO LITTLE KNIGHTS OF

By

ANNIE FELLOWS JOHNSTON

CHAPTER I.

TWO TRAMPS AND A BEAR.

It was the coldest Saint Valentine's eve that Kentucky had known in twenty years. In Lloydsborough Valley a thin sprinkling of snow whitened the meadows, enough to show the footprints of every hungry rabbit that loped across them; but there were not many such tracks. It was so cold that the rabbits, for all their thick fur, were glad to run home and hide. Nobody cared to be out long in such weather, and except now and then, when an ice-cutter's wagon creaked up from some pond to the frozen pike, the wintry stillness was unbroken.

On the north side of the little country depot a long row of icicles hung from the eaves. Even the wind seemed to catch its breath there, and hurry on with a shiver that reached to the telegraph wires overhead. It shivered down the long stovepipe, too, inside the waiting-room. The stove had been kept red-hot all that dull gray afternoon, but the window-panes were still white with heavy frost-work.

Half an hour before the five o'clock train was due from the city, two boys came running up the railroad track with their skates in their hands. They were handsome, sturdy little fellows, so well buttoned up in their leather leggins and warm reefer overcoats that they scarcely felt the cold. Their cheeks were red as winter apples, from skating against the wind, and they were almost breathless after their long run up-hill to the depot. Racing across the platform, they bumped against the door at the same instant, burst it noisily open, and slammed it behind them with a bang that shook the entire building.

"What kind of a cyclone has struck us now?" growled the ticket agent, who was in the next room. Then he frowned, as the first noise was followed by the rasping sound of a bench being dragged out of a corner, to a place nearer the stove. It scraped the bare floor every inch of the way, with a jarring motion that made the windows rattle.

Stretching himself half-way out of his chair, the ticket agent pushed up the wooden slide of the little window far enough for him to peep into the waiting-room. Then he hastily shoved it down again.

"It's the two little chaps who came out from the city last week," he said to the station-master. "The MacIntyre boys. You'd think they own the earth from the way they dash in and take possession of things."

The station-master liked boys. He stroked his gray beard and chuckled. "Well, Meyers," he said, slowly, "when you come to think of it, their family always has owned a pretty fair slice of the earth and its good things, and those same little lads have travelled nearly all over it, although the oldest can't be more than ten. It would be a wonder if they didn't have that lordly way of making themselves at home wherever they go."

"Will they be out here all winter?" asked Meyers, who was a newcomer in Lloydsborough.

"Yes, their father and mother have gone to Florida, and left them here with their grandmother MacIntyre."

"I imagine the old lady has her hands full," said Meyers, as a sound of scuffling in the next room reached him.

"Oh, I don't know about that, now," said the station-master. "They're noisy children, to be sure, and just boiling over with mischief, but if you can find any better-mannered little gentlemen anywhere in the State when there's ladies around, I'd like you to trot 'em out. They came down to the train with their aunt this morning, Miss Allison MacIntyre, and their politeness to her was something pretty to see, I can tell you, sir."

There was a moment's pause, in which the boys could be heard laughing in the next room.

"No," said the station-master again, "I'm thinking it's not the boys who will be keeping Mrs. MacIntyre's hands full this winter, so much as that little granddaughter of hers that came here last fall,--little Virginia Dudley. You can guess what's she like from her nickname. They call her Ginger. She had always lived at some army post out West, until her father, Captain Dudley, was ordered to Cuba. He was wounded down there, and has never been entirely well since. When he found they were going to keep him there all winter, he sent for his wife last September, and there was nothing to do with Virginia but to bring her back to Kentucky to her grandmother."

"Oh, she's the little girl who went in on the train this morning with Miss Allison," said the ticket agent. "I suppose the boys have come down to meet them. They'll have a long time to wait."

While this conversation was going on behind the ticket window, the two boys stretched themselves out on a long bench beside the stove. The warm room made them feel drowsy after their violent out-door exercise. Keith, the younger one, yawned several times, and finally lay down on the bench with his cap for a pillow. He was eight years old, but curled up in that fashion, with his long eyelashes resting on his red cheeks, and one plump little hand tucked under his chin, he looked much younger.

"Wake me up, Malcolm, when it's time for Aunt Allison's train," he said to his brother. "Ginger would never stop teasing me if she should find me asleep."

Malcolm unbuttoned his reefer, and, after much tugging, pulled out a handsome little gold watch. "Oh, there's a long time to wait!" he exclaimed. "We need not have left the pond so early, for the train will not be here for twenty-five minutes. I believe I'll curl up here myself, till then. I hope they won't forget the valentines we sent for."

The room was very still for a few minutes. There was no sound at all except the crackling of the fire and the shivering of the wind in the long stovepipe. Then some one turned the door-knob so cautiously and slowly that it unlatched without a sound.

It was the cold air rushing into the room as the door was pushed ajar that aroused the boys. After one surprised glance they sat up, for the man, who was slipping into the room as stealthily as a burglar, was the worst-looking tramp they had ever seen. There was a long, ugly red scar across his face, running from his cheek to the middle of his forehead, and partly closing one eye. Perhaps it was the scar that gave him such a queer, evil sort of an expression; even without it he would have been a repulsive sight. His clothes were dirty and ragged, and his breath had frozen in icicles on his stubby red beard.

Behind him came a boy no larger than Keith, but with a hard, shrewd look in his hungry little face that made one feel he had lived a long time and learned more than was good for him to know. It was plain to be seen that he was nearly starved, and suffering from the intense cold. His bare toes peeped through their ragged shoes, and he had no coat. A thin cotton shirt and a piece of an old gray horse-blanket was all that protected his shoulders from the icy wind of that February afternoon. He, too, crept in noiselessly, as if expecting to be ordered out at the first sound, and then turned to coax in some animal that was tied to one end of the rope which he held.

Malcolm and Keith looked on with interest, and sprang up excitedly as the animal finally shuffled in far enough for the boy to close the door behind it. It was a great, shaggy bear, taller than the man when it sat up on its haunches beside him.

The tramp looked uneasily around the room for an instant, but seeing no one save the two children, ventured nearer the stove. The boy followed him, and the bear shuffled along behind them both, limping painfully. Not a word was said for a moment. The boys were casting curious glances at the three tramps who had come in as noiselessly as if they had snowed down, and the man was watching the boys with shrewd eyes. He did not seem to be looking at them, but at the end of his survey he could have described them accurately. He had noticed every detail of their clothing, from their expensive leather leggins to their fur-lined gloves. He glanced at Malcolm's watch-chain and the fine skates which Keith swung back and forth by a strap, and made up his mind, correctly, too, that the pockets of these boys rarely lacked the jingle of money which they could spend as they pleased.

When he turned away to hold his hands out toward the stove, he rubbed them together with satisfaction, for he had discovered more than that. He knew from their faces that they were trusting little souls, who would believe any story he might tell them, if he appealed to their sympathies in the right way. He was considering how to begin, when Malcolm broke the silence.

"Is that a trained bear?"

The man nodded.

"What can it do?" was the next question.

"Oh, lots of things," answered the man, in a low, whining voice. "Drill like a soldier, and dance, and ride a stick." He kept his shifty eyes turning constantly toward the door, as if afraid some one might overhear him.

"I'd put him through his paces for you young gen'lemen," he said, "but he got his foot hurt for one thing, and another is, if we went to showing off, we might be ordered to move on. This is the first time we've smelled a fire in twenty-four hours, and we ain't in no hurry to leave it, I can tell you."

"Will he bite?" asked Keith, going up to the huge bear, which had stretched itself out comfortably on the floor.

"Not generally. He's a good-tempered brute, most times like a lamb. But he ain't had nothing to eat all day, so it wouldn't be surprising if he was a bit snappish."

"Nothing to eat!" echoed Keith. "You poor old thing!" Going a step closer, he put out his hand and stroked the bear, as if it had been a great dog.

"Oh, Malcolm, just feel how soft his fur is, like mamma's beaver jacket. And he has the kindest old face. Poor old fellow, is you hungry? Never mind, Keith'll get you something to eat pretty soon."

Putting his short, plump arms around the animal's neck, he hugged it lovingly up to him. A cunning gleam came into the man's eyes. He saw that he had gained the younger boy's sympathy, and he wanted Malcolm's also.

"Is your home near here, my little gen'leman?" he asked, in a friendly tone.

"No, we live in the city," answered Malcolm, "but my grandmother's place, where we are staying, is not far from here." He was stroking the bear with one hand as he spoke, and hunting in his pocket with the other, hoping to find some stray peanuts to give it.

"Then maybe you know of some place where we could stay to-night. Even a shed to crawl into would keep us from freezing. It's an awful cold night not to have a roof over your head, or a crust to gnaw on, or a spark of fire to keep life in your body."

"Maybe they'd let you stay in the waiting-room," suggested Malcolm. "It is always good and warm in here. I'll ask the station-master. He's a friend of mine."

"Oh, no! No, don't!" exclaimed the tramp, hastily, pulling his old hat farther over his forehead, as if to hide the scar, and looking uneasily around. "I wouldn't have you do that for anything. I've had dealings with such folks before, and I know how they'd treat *me*. I thought maybe there was a barn or a hay-shed or something on your grandmother's place, where we could lay up for repairs a couple of days. The beast needs a rest. Its foot's sore; and Jonesy there is pretty near to lung fever, judging from the way he coughs." He nodded toward the boy, who had placed his chair as close to the stove as possible. The child's face was drawn into a pucker by the tingling pains in his half-frozen feet, and his efforts to keep from coughing.

Malcolm looked at him steadily. He had read about boys who were homeless and hungry and cold, but he had never really understood how much it meant to be all that. This was the first time in his ten short years that he had ever come close to real poverty. He had seen the swarms of beggars that infest such cities as Naples and Rome, and had tossed them coppers because that seemed a part of the programme in travelling. He had not really felt sorry for them, for they did not seem to mind it. They sat on the steps in the warm Italian sunshine, and waited for tourists to throw them money, as comfortably as toads sit blinking at flies. But this was different. A wave of pity swept through Malcolm's generous little heart as he looked at Jonesy, and the man watching him shrewdly saw it.

"Of course," he whined, "a little gen'leman like you don't know what it is to go from town to town and have every door shut in your face. You don't think that this is a hard-hearted, stingy old world, because it has given you the cream of everything. But if you'd never had anything all your life but other people's scraps and leavings, and you hadn't any home or friends or money, and was sick besides, you'd think things wasn't very evenly divided. Wouldn't you now? You'd think it wasn't right that some should have all that heart can wish, and others not enough to keep soul and body together. If you'd-a happened to be Jonesy, and Jonesy had a-happened to 'a' been you, I reckon you'd feel it was pretty tough to see such a big difference between you. It doesn't seem fair now, does it?"

"No," admitted Malcolm, faintly. He had taken a dislike to the man. He could not have told why, but his child instinct armed him with a sudden distrust. Still, he felt the force of the whining appeal, and the burden of an obligation to help them seemed laid upon his shoulders.

"Grandmother is afraid for anybody to sleep in the barn, on account of fire," he said, after a moment's thought, "and I'm sure she wouldn't let you come into the house without you'd had a bath and some clean clothes. Grandmother is dreadfully particular," he added, hastily, not wanting to be impolite even to a tramp. "Seems to me Keith and I have to spend half our time washing our hands and putting on clean collars."

"Oh, I know a place," cried Keith. "There's that empty cabin down by the spring-house. Nobody has lived in it since the new servants' cottage was built. There isn't any furniture in it, but there's a fireplace in one room, and it would be warmer than the barn."

"That's just the trick!" exclaimed Malcolm. "We can carry a pile of hay over from the barn for you to sleep on. Aunt Allison will be out on this next train and I'll ask her. I am sure she will let you, because last night, when it was so cold, she said she felt sorry for anything that had to be out in it, even the poor old cedar trees, with the sleet on their branches. She said that it was King Lear's own weather, and she could understand how Cordelia felt when she said, *'Mine enemy's dog, though he had bit me, should have stood that night against my fire!'* It is just like auntie to feel that way about it, only she's so good to everybody she couldn't have any enemies."

Something like a smile moved the tramp's stubby beard. "So she's that kind, is she? Well, if she could have a soft spot for a dog that had bit her, and an enemy's dog at that, it stands to reason that she wouldn't object to some harmless travellers a-sleeping in an empty cabin a couple of nights. S'pose'n you show us the place, sonny, and we'll be moving on."

"Oh, it wouldn't be right not to ask her first," exclaimed Malcolm. "She'll be here in such a little while."

The man looked uneasy. Presently he walked over to the window and scraped a peep-hole on the frosted pane with his dirty thumbnail. "Sun's down," he said. "I'd like to get that bear's foot fixed comfortable before it grows any darker. I'd like to mighty well. It'll take some time to heat water to dress it. Is that cabin far from here?"

"Not if we go in at the back of the place," said Malcolm. "It's just across the meadow, and over a little hill. If we went around by the big front gate it would be a good deal longer."

The man shifted uneasily from one foot to another, and complained of being hungry. He was growing desperate. For more reasons than one he did not want to be at the station when the train came in. That long red scar across his face had been described a number of times in the newspapers, and he did not care to be recognised just then.

The boys could not have told how it came about, but in a few minutes they were leading the way toward the cabin. The man had persuaded them that it was not at all necessary to wait for their Aunt Allison's permission, and that it was needless to trouble their grandmother. Why should the ladies be bothered about a matter that the boys were old enough to decide? So well had he argued, and so tactfully had he flattered them, that when they took their way across the field, it was with the feeling that they were doing their highest duty in getting these homeless wayfarers to the cabin as quickly as possible, on their own responsibility.

"ACROSS THE SNOWY FIELDS."

"We can get back in time to meet the train, if we hurry," said Malcolm, looking at his watch again. "There's still fifteen minutes."

No one saw the little procession file out of the waiting-room and across the snowy field, for it was growing dark, and the lamps were lighted and the curtains drawn in the few houses they passed. Malcolm went first, proudly leading the friendly old bear. Jonesy came next beside Keith, and the man shuffled along in the rear, looking around with suspicious glances whenever a twig snapped, or a distant dog barked.

As the wind struck against Jonesy's body, he drew the bit of blanket more closely around him, and coughed hoarsely. His teeth were chattering and his lips blue. "You look nearly frozen," said Keith, who, well-clad and well-fed, scarcely felt the cold. "Here! put this on, or you'll be sick," Unbuttoning his thick little reefer, he pulled it off and tied its sleeves around Jonesy's neck.

A strange look passed over the face of the man behind them. "Blessed if the little kid didn't take it off his own back," he muttered. "If any man had ever done that for me--just once--well, maybe, I wouldn't ha' been what I am now!"

For a moment, as they reached the top of the hill, bear, boys, and man were outlined blackly against the sky like strange silhouettes. Then they passed over and disappeared in the thick clump of pine-trees, which hid the little cabin from the eyes of the surrounding world.

CHAPTER II.

GINGER AND THE BOYS.

In less time than one would think possible, a big fire was roaring in the cabin fireplace, water was steaming in the rusty kettle on the crane, and a pile of hay and old carpet lay in one corner, ready to be made into a bed. Keith had made several trips to the kitchen, and came back each time with his hands full.

Old Daphne, the cook, never could find it in her heart to refuse "Marse Sydney's" boys anything. They were too much like what their father had been at their age to resist their playful coaxing. She had nursed him when he was a baby, and had been his loyal champion all through his boyhood. Now her black face wrinkled into smiles whenever she heard his name spoken. In her eyes, nobody was quite so near perfection as he, except, perhaps, the fair woman whom he had married.

"Kain't nobody in ten States hole a can'le to my Marse Sidney an' his Miss Elise," old Daphne used to say, proudly. "They sut'n'ly is the handsomest couple evah jined togethah, an' the free-handedest. In all they travels by sea or by land they nevah fo'gits ole Daphne. I've got things from every country undah the shinin' sun what they done brung me."

Now, all the services she had once been proud to render them were willingly given to their little sons. When Keith came in with a pitiful tale of a tramp who was starving at their very gates, she gave him even more than he asked for, and almost more than he could carry.

The bear and its masters were so hungry, and their two little hosts so interested in watching them eat, that they forgot all about going back to meet the train. They did not even hear it whistle when it came puffing into the Valley.

As Miss Allison stepped from the car to the station platform, she looked around in vain for the boys who had promised to meet her. Her arms were so full of bundles, as suburban passengers' usually are, that she could not hold up her long broadcloth skirt, or even turn her handsome fur collar higher over her ears. With a shade of annoyance on her pretty face, she swept across the platform and into the waiting-room, out of the cold.

Behind her came a little girl about ten years old, as unlike her as possible, although it was Virginia Dudley's ambition to be exactly like her Aunt Allison. She wanted to be tall, and slender, and grown up; Miss Allison was that, and yet she had kept all her lively girlish ways, and a love of fun that made her charming to everybody, young and old. Virginia longed for wavy brown hair and white hands, and especially for a graceful, easy manner. Her hair was short and black, and her complexion like a gypsy's. She had hard, brown little fists, sharp gray eyes that seemed to see everything at once, and a tongue that was always getting her into trouble. As for the ease of manner, that might come in time, but her stately old grandmother often sighed in secret over Virginia's awkwardness.

She stumbled now as she followed the young lady into the waiting-room. Her big, plume-covered hat tipped over one ear, but she, too, had so many bundles, that she could not spare a hand to straighten it.

"Well, Virginia, what do you suppose has become of the boys?" asked her aunt. "They promised to meet us and carry our packages."

"I heard them in here about half an hour ago, Miss Allison," said the station-master, who had come in with a lantern. "I s'pose they got tired of waiting. Better leave your things here, hadn't you? I'll watch them. It is mighty slippery walking this evening."

"Oh, thank you, Mr. Mason," she answered, beginning to pile boxes and packages upon a bench, I'll send Pete down for them immediately. Now, Virginia, turn up your coat collar and hold your muff over your nose, or Jack Frost will make an icicle out of you before you are half-way home.

They had been in the house some time before the boys remembered their promise to meet them at the station. When they saw how late it was, they started home on the run.

"I am fairly aching to tell Ginger about that bear," panted Keith, as they reached the side door. "I am so sorry that we promised the man not to say anything about them being on the place, before he sees us again to-morrow. I wonder why he asked us that."

"I don't know," answered Malcolm. "He seemed to have some very good reason, and he talked about it so that it didn't seem right not to promise a little thing like that."

"I wish we hadn't, though," said Keith, again.

"But it's done now," persisted Malcolm. "We're bound not to tell, and you can't get out of it, for he made us give him our word 'on the honour of a gentleman;' and that settles it, you know."

They were two very dirty boys who clattered up the back stairs, and raced to their room to dress for dinner. Their clothes were covered with hayseed and straw, and their hands and faces were black with soot from the old cabin chimney. They had both helped to build the fire.

The lamps had just been lighted in the upper hall, and Virginia came running out from her room when she heard the boys' voices.

"Why didn't you meet us at the train?" she began, but stopped as she saw their dirty faces. "Where on earth have you chimney-sweeps been?" she cried.

"Oh, about and about," answered Malcolm, teasingly. "Don't you wish you knew?"

Virginia shrugged her shoulders, as if she had not the slightest interest in the matter, and held out two packages.

"Here are the valentines you sent for. You just ought to see the pile that Aunt Allison bought. We've the best secret about to-morrow that ever was."

"So have we," began Keith, but Malcolm clapped a sooty hand over his mouth and pulled him toward the door of their room. "Come on," he said. "We've barely time to dress for dinner. Don't you know enough to keep still, you little magpie?" he exclaimed, as the door banged behind them. "The only way to keep a secret is not to act like you have one!"

Virginia walked slowly back to her room and paused in the doorway, wondering what she could do to amuse herself until dinner-time. It was a queer room for a girl, decorated with flags and

Indian trophies and everything that could remind her of the military life she loved, at the faraway army post. There were photographs framed in brass buttons on her dressing-table, and pictures of uniformed officers all over the walls. A canteen and an army cap with a bullet-hole through the crown, hung over her desk, and a battered bugle, that had sounded many a triumphant charge, swung from the corner of her mirror.

Each souvenir had a history, and had been given her at parting by some special friend. Every one at the fort had made a pet of Captain Dudley's daughter,--the harum-scarum little Ginger,--who would rather dash across the prairies on her pony, like a wild Comanche Indian, than play with the finest doll ever imported from Paris.

There was a suit in her wardrobe, short skirt, jacket, leggins, and moccasins, all made and beaded by the squaws. It was the gift of the colonel's wife. Mrs. Dudley had hesitated some time before putting it in one of the trunks that was to go back to Kentucky.

"You look so much like an Indian now," she said to Virginia. "Your face is so sunburned that I am afraid your grandmother will be scandalised. I don't know what she would say if she knew that I ever allowed you to run so wild. If I had known that you were going back to civilisation I certainly should not have kept your hair cut short, and you should have worn sunbonnets all summer."

To Mrs. Dudley's great surprise, her little daughter threw herself into her arms, sobbing, "Oh, mamma! I don't want to go back to Kentucky! Take me to Cuba with you! Please do, or else let me stay here at the post. Everybody will take care of me here! I'll just *die* if you leave me in Kentucky!"

"Why, darling," she said, soothingly, as she wiped her tears away and rocked her back and forth in her arms, "I thought you have always wanted to see mamma's old home, and the places you have heard so much about. There are all the old toys in the nursery that we had when we were children, and the grape-vine swing in the orchard, and the mill-stream where we fished, and the beech-woods where we had such delightful picnics. I thought it would be so nice for you to do all the same things that made me so happy when I was a child, and go to school in the same old Girls' College and know all the dear old neighbours that I knew. Wouldn't my little girl like that?"

"Oh, yes, some, I s'pose," sobbed Virginia, "but I didn't know I'd have to be so--so--everlastingly--civilised!" she wailed. "I don't want to always have to dress just so, and have to walk in a path and be called Virginia all the time. That sounds so stiff and proper. I'd rather stay where people don't mind if I am sunburned and tanned, and won't be scandalised at everything I do. It's so much nicer to be just plain Ginger!"

It had been five months, now, since Virginia left Fort Dennis. At first she had locked hen self in her room nearly every day, and, with her face buried in her Indian suit, cried to go back. She missed the gay military life of the army post, as a sailor would miss the sea, or an Alpine shepherd the free air of his snow-capped mountain heights.

It was not that she did not enjoy being at her grandmother's. She liked the great gray house whose square corner tower and over-hanging vines made it look like an old castle. She liked the comfort and elegance of the big, stately rooms, and she had her grandmother's own pride in the old family portraits and the beautiful carved furniture. The negro servants seemed so queer and funny to her that she found them a great source of amusement, and her Aunt Allison planned so many pleasant occupations outside of school-hours that she scarcely had time to get lonesome. But she had a shut-in feeling, like a wild bird in a cage, and sometimes the longing for liberty which her mother had allowed her made her fret against the thousand little proprieties she had to observe. Sometimes when she went tipping over the polished floors of the long drawing room, and caught sight of herself in one of the big mirrors, she felt that she was not herself at all, but somebody in a story. The Virginia in the looking-glass seemed so very, very civilised. More than once, after one of these meetings with herself in the mirror, she dashed up-stairs, locked her door, and dressed herself in her Indian suit. Then in her noiseless moccasins she danced the wildest of war-dances, whispering shrilly between her teeth, "Now I'm Ginger! Now I'm Ginger! And I *won't* be dressed up, and I *won't* learn my lessons, and I *won't* be a little lady, and I'll run away and go back to Fort Dennis the very first chance I get!"

Usually she was ashamed of these outbursts afterwards, for it always happened that after each one she found her Aunt Allison had planned something especially pleasant for her entertainment. Miss Allison felt sorry for the lonely child, who had never been separated from her father and mother before, so she devoted her time to her as much as possible, telling her stories and entering into her plays and pleasures as if they had both been the same age.

Since the boys had come, Virginia had not had a single homesick moment. While she was at school in the primary department of the Girls' College, Malcolm and Keith were reciting their lessons to the old minister who lived across the road from Mrs. MacIntyre's. They were all free about the same hour, and even on the coldest days played out-of-doors from lunch-time until dark.

To-night Virginia had so many experiences to tell them of her day in town that the boys seemed unusually long in dressing. She was so impatient for them to hear her news that she could not settle down to anything, but walked restlessly around the room, wishing they would hurry.

"Oh, I haven't sorted my valentines!" she exclaimed, presently, picking up a fancy box which she had tossed on the bed when she first came in. "I'll take them down to the library."

There was no one in the room when she peeped in. It looked so bright and cosy with the great wood fire blazing on the hearth and the rose-coloured light falling from its softly shaded lamps, that she forgot the coldness of the night outside. Sitting down on a pile of cushions at one end of the hearth-rug, she began sorting her purchases, trying to decide to whom each one should be sent.

"The prettiest valentine of all must go to poor papa," she said to herself, "'cause he's been so sick away down there in Cuba; and this one that's got the little girl on it in a blue dress shall be for my dear, sweet mamma, 'cause it will make her think of me."

For a moment, a mist seemed to blur the gay blue dress of the little valentine girl as Virginia looked at her, thinking of her far-away mother. She drew her hand hastily across her eyes and went on:

"This one is for Sergeant Jackson out at Fort Dennis, and the biggest one, with the doves, for Colonel Philips and his wife. Dear me! I wish I could send one to every officer and soldier out there. They were all *so* good to me!"

The pile of lace-paper cupids and hearts and arrows and roses slipped from her lap, down to the rug, as she clasped her hands around her knees and looked into the fire. She wished that she could be back again at the fort, long enough to live one of those beautiful old days from reveille to taps. How she loved the bugle-calls and the wild thrill the band gave her, when it struck up a burst of martial music, and the troops went dashing by! How she missed the drills and the dress parades; her rides across the open prairie on her pony, beside her father; how she missed the games she used to play with the other children at the fort on the long summer evenings!

Something more than a mist was gathering in her eyes now. Two big tears were almost ready to fall when the door opened and Mrs. MacIntyre came in. In Virginia's eyes she was the most beautiful grandmother any one ever had. She was not so tall as her daughter Allison, and in that respect fell short of the little girl's ideal, but her hair, white as snow, curled around her face in the same soft, pretty fashion, and by every refined feature she showed her kinship to the aristocratic old faces which looked down from the family portraits in the hall.

"I couldn't be as stately and dignified as she is if I practised a thousand years," thought Virginia, scrambling up from the pile of cushions to roll a chair nearer the fire. As she did so, her heel caught in the rug, and she fell back in an awkward little heap.

"The more haste, the less grace, my dear," said her grandmother, kindly, thanking her for the proffered chair. Virginia blushed, wondering why she always appeared so awkward in her grandmother's presence. She envied the boys because they never seemed embarrassed or ill at ease before her.

While she was picking up her valentines the boys came in. If two of the cavalier ancestors had stepped down from their portrait frames just then, they could not have come into the room in a more charming manner than Malcolm and Keith. Their faces were shining, their linen spotless, and they came up to kiss their grandmother's cheek with an old-time courtliness that delighted her.

"I am sure that there are no more perfect gentlemen in all Kentucky than my two little lads," she said, fondly, with an approving pat of Keith's hand as she held him a moment.

Virginia, who had seen them half an hour before, tousled and dirty, and had been arrayed against them in more than one hot quarrel where they had been anything but chivalrous, let slip a faintly whistled "*cuckoo!*"

The boys darted a quick glance in her direction, but she was bending over the valentines with a very serious face, which never changed its expression till her Aunt Allison came in and the boys began their apologies for not meeting her at the train. Their only excuse was that they had forgotten all about it.

Virginia spelled on her fingers: "I dare you to tell what made your faces so black!" Keith's only answer was to thrust his tongue out at her behind his grandmother's back. Then he ran to hold the door open for the ladies to pass out to dinner, with all the grace of a young Chesterfield.

When dinner was over and they were back in the library, Miss Allison opened a box of tiny heart-shaped envelopes, and began addressing them. As she took up her pen she said, merrily: "*Now* you may tell our secret, Virginia."

"I was going to make you guess for about an hour," said Virginia, "but it is so nice I can't wait that long to tell you. We are going to have a valentine party to-morrow night. Aunt Allison planned it all a week ago, and bought the things for it while we were in town to-day. Everything on the table is to be cut in heart shape,--the bread and butter and sandwiches and cheese; and the ice-cream will be moulded in hearts, and the two big frosted cakes are hearts, one pink and one white, with candy arrows sticking in them. Then there will be peppermint candy hearts with mottoes printed on them, and lace-paper napkins with verses on them, so that the table itself will look like a lovely big valentine. The games are lovely, too. One is parlour archery, with a red heart in the middle of the target, and two prizes, one for the boys and one for the girls."

"Who are invited?" asked Malcolm, as Virginia stopped for breath.

"Oh, the Carrington boys, and the Edmunds, and Sally Fairfax, and Julia Ferris,--I can't remember them all. There will be twenty-four, counting us. There is the list on the table."

Keith reached for it, and began slowly spelling out the names. "Who is this?" he asked, reading the name that headed the list. "'The Little Colonel!' I never heard of him,"

"Oh, he's a girl!" laughed Virginia. Little Lloyd Sherman,--don't you know? She lives up at 'The Locusts,' that lovely place with the long avenue of trees leading up to the house. You've surely seen her with her grandfather, old Colonel Lloyd, riding by on the horse that he calls Maggie Boy."

"Has he only one arm?" asked Malcolm.

"Yes, the other was shot off in the war years ago. Well, when Lloyd was younger, she had a temper so much like his, and wore such a dear little Napoleon hat, that everybody took to calling her the Little Colonel."

"How old is she now?" asked Malcolm.

"About Keith's age, isn't she, Aunt Allison?" asked Virginia.

"Yes," was the answer. "She is nearly eight, I believe. She has outgrown most of her naughtiness now."

"I love to hear her talk," said Virginia. "She leaves out all of her r's in such a soft, sweet way."

"All Southerners do that," said Malcolm, pompously, "and I think it sounds lots better than the way Yankees talk."

"You boys don't talk like the Little Colonel," retorted Virginia, who had often been teased by them for not being a Southerner. "You're all mixed up every which way. Some things you say like darkeys, and some things like English people, and it doesn't sound a bit like the Little Colonel."

"Oh, well, that's because we've travelled abroad so much, don't you know," drawled Malcolm, "and we've been in so many different countries, and had an English tutor, and all that sort of a thing. We couldn't help picking up a bit of an accent, don't you know." His superior tone made Virginia long to slap him.

"Yes, I know, Mr. Brag," she said, in such a low voice that her grandmother could not hear. "I know perfectly well. If I didn't it wouldn't be because you haven't told me every chance you got. Who did you say is your tailor in London, and how many times was it the Queen invited you out to Windsor? I think it's a ninety-nine dollar cravat you always buy, isn't it? And you wouldn't be so common as to wear a pair of gloves that hadn't been made to order specially for you. Yes, I've heard all about it!"

Miss Allison heard, but said nothing. She knew the boys were a little inclined to boast, and she thought Virginia's sharp tongue might have a good effect. But the retort had grown somewhat sharper than was pleasant, and, fearing a quarrel might follow if she did not interrupt the whispers beside her, she said:

"Boys, did you ever hear about the time that the Little Colonel threw mud on her grandfather's coat? There's no end to her pranks. Get grandmother to tell you."

"Oh, yes, please, grandmother," begged Keith, with an arm around her neck. "Tell about Fritz and the parrot, too," said Virginia. "Here, Malcolm, there's room on this side for you."

Aunt Allison smiled. The storm had blown over, and they were all friends again.

"'DAPHNE, WHAT'S DEM CHILLUN ALLUZ RACIN' DOWN TO DE SPRING-HOUSE FO'?'"

CHAPTER III.

THE VALENTINE PARTY.

"Now we can tell Ginger about the bear," was Keith's first remark, when he awoke early next morning.

"But not until after we have seen the man again," answered Malcolm. "You know we promised him that."

"Then let's go down before breakfast," exclaimed Keith, springing out of bed and beginning to dress himself. A little while later, the old coloured coachman saw them run past the window, where he was warming himself by the kitchen stove.

"Daphne," he called out to the cook, who was beating biscuit in the adjoining pantry, "Daphne, what's dem chillun alluz racin' down to de spring-house fo' in de snow? Peah's lak dee has a heap o' business down yandah."

Daphne, who had just been coaxed into filling a basket with a generous supply of cold victuals, pretended not to hear until he repeated his question. Then she stopped pounding long enough to say, sharply, "Whuffo' you alluz 'spicion dem boys so evahlastin'ly, Unc' Henry? Lak enough dee's settin' a rabbit trap. Boys has done such things befo'. You's done it yo'se'f, hasn't you?"

Daphne had seen them setting rabbit traps there, but she knew well enough that was not what they had gone for now, and that the food they carried was not for the game of Robinson Crusoe, which they had played in the deserted cabin the summer before. Still, she did not care to take Unc' Henry into her confidence.

The food, the warmth, and the night's rest had so restored the bear that it was able to go through all its performances for the boys' entertainment, although it limped badly.

"Isn't he a dandy?" cried Keith; "I wish we had one. It's nicer than any pets we ever had, except the ponies. Something always happened to the dogs, and the monkey was such a nuisance, and the white rabbits were stolen, and the guinea pigs died."

"Haven't we had a lot of things, when you come to think of it?" exclaimed Malcolm. "Squirrels, and white mice, and the coon that Uncle Harry brought us, and the parrot from Mexico."

"Yes, and the gold-fish, and the little baby alligator that froze to death in its tank," added Keith. "But a bear like this would be nicer than any of them. As soon as papa comes home I am going to ask him to buy us one."

"Jonesy's nearly done for," said the tramp, pointing to the boy who lay curled up in the hay, coughing at nearly every breath. "We ought to stay here another day, if you young gen'lemen don't object."

"Oh, goody!" cried Keith. "Then we can bring Ginger down to see the bear perform."

"Yes," answered the man, "we'll give a free show to all your friends, if you will only kindly wait till to-morrow. Give us one more day to rest up and get in a little better trim. The poor beast's foot is still too lame for him to do his best, and you're too kind-hearted, I am sure, to want anything to suffer in order to give you pleasure."

"Of course," answered both the boys, agreeing so quickly to all the man's smooth speeches that, before they left the cabin, they had renewed their promise to keep silent one more day. The man was a shrewd one, and knew well how to make these unsuspecting little souls serve his purpose, like puppets tied to a string.

Miss Allison was so busy with preparations for the party that she had no time all that day to notice what the boys were doing. When they came back from reciting their lessons to the minister, she sent them on several errands, but the rest of the time they divided between the cabin and the post-office.

Every mail brought a few valentines to each of them, but it was not until the five o'clock train came that they found the long-looked-for letters from their father and mother.

"I knew they'd each send us a valentine," cried Keith, tearing both of his open. "I'll bet that papa's is a comic one. Yes, here it is. Papa is such a tease. Isn't it a stunner? a base-ball player. And, whoopee! Here's a dollar bill in each of 'em."

"So there is in mine," said Malcolm. "Mamma says we are to buy anything we want, and call it a valentine. They couldn't find anything down on the coast that they thought we would like."

"I don't know what to get with mine," said Keith, folding his two bills together. "Seems to me I have everything I want except a camera, and I couldn't buy the kind I want for two dollars."

They were half-way home when a happy thought came to Malcolm. "Keith," he cried, excitedly, "if you would put your money with mine, that would make four dollars, and maybe it would be enough to buy that bear!"

"Let's do it!" exclaimed Keith, turning a handspring in the snow to show his delight. "Come on, we'll ask the man now."

But the man shook his head, when they dashed into the cabin and told their errand. "No, sonny, that ain't a tenth of what it's worth to me," he said. "I've raised that bear from the time it was a teeny cub. I've taught it, and fed it, and looked to it for company when I hadn't nobody in the world to care for me. Couldn't sell that bear for no such sum as that. Couldn't you raise any more money than that?"

It was Malcolm's turn to shake his head. He turned away, too disappointed to trust himself to answer any other way. The tears sprang to Keith's eyes. He had set his heart on having that bear.

"Never mind, brother," said Malcolm, moving toward the door. "Papa will get us one when he comes home and finds how much we want one."

"Oh, don't be in such a hurry, young gen'lemen," whined the man, when he saw that they were really going. "I didn't say that I wouldn't sell it to you for that much. You've been so kind to me that I ought to be willing to make any sacrifice for you. I happen to need four dollars very particular just now, and I've a mind to sell him to you on your own terms." He paused a moment, looking thoughtfully at a crack in the floor, as he stood by the fire with his hands in his pockets. "Yes," he said, at last, "you can have him for four dollars, if you'll keep mum about us being here for one more day. You can leave the bear here till we go."

"No! No!" cried Keith, throwing his arms around the animal's neck. "He is ours now, and we must take him with us. We can hide him away in the barn. It is so dark out-doors now that nobody will see us. It wouldn't seem like he is really ours if we couldn't take him with us."

After some grumbling the man consented, and pocketed the four dollars, first asking very particularly the exact spot in the barn where they expected to hide their huge pet.

Unc' Henry, coming up from the carriage-house through the twilight, thought he saw some one stealing along by the clump of cedars by the spring-house. "Who's prowlin' roun' dis yere premises?" he called. There was no answer, and, after peering intently through the dusk for a moment, the old darkey concluded that he must have been mistaken, and passed on. As soon as he was gone, the boys came out from behind the cedars, and crept up the snowy hillside. They were leading the bear between them.

"We'll put him away back in the hay-mow where he'll be warm and comfortable to-night," whispered Malcolm. "Then in the morning we can tell everybody."

While they were busily scooping out a big hollow in the hay, they were startled by a rustling behind them. They looked into each other's frightened faces, and then glanced around the dark barn in alarm. An old cap pushed up through the hay. Then a weak little cough betrayed Jonesy. He had followed them.

"Sh!" he said, in a warning whisper. "I'm afraid the boss will find out that I'm here. He started to the store for some tobacco as soon as you left. He's been wild fer some, but didn't have no money. *Don't you leave that bear out here to-night, if you ever expect to see it again!* That wasn't true what he told you. He never saw the bear till two months ago, and he sold it to you cheap because he's a-goin' to steal it back again to-night, and make off up the road with it. He went off a-grinnin' over the slick way he'd fooled you, and I jes' had to come and tell, 'cause you've been so good to me. I'll never forget the little kid's givin' me the coat off his own back, if I live to be a hundred. Now don't blab on me, or the boss would nearly kill me."

"Is that man your father?" began Keith, but Jonesy, alarmed by some sudden noise, sprang to the door, and disappeared in the twilight.

The boys looked at each other a moment, with surprise and indignation in their faces. There was a hurried consultation in the hay-mow. A few moments later the boys were smuggling their new pet into the house, and up the back stairs. They scarcely dared breathe until it was safe in their own room.

All the time that they were dressing for the party, they were trying to decide where to put it for the night, so that neither the tramp nor the family could discover it. What Jonesy had told them about the man's dishonest intention did not relieve them from their promise. They were amazed that any one could be so mean, and longed to tell their Aunt Allison all about it; still, one of the conditions on which they had bought the bear was that they were to "keep mum," and they stuck strictly to that promise.

By the time they were dressed, they had decided to put it in the blue room, a guest-chamber in the north wing, seldom used in winter, because it was so hard to heat. "Nobody will ever think of coming in here," said Malcolm, "and it will be plenty warm for a bear if we turn on the furnace a little." As he spoke, he was tying the bear's rope around a leg of the big, high-posted bed.

"Won't Ginger be surprised?" answered Keith. "We'll tell her that we have a valentine six feet long, and keep her guessing."

There was no time for teasing, however, as the first guest arrived while they were still in the blue room.

"I hate to go off and leave him in the dark," said Keith, with a final loving pat. "I guess he'll not mind, though. Maybe he'll think he is in the woods if I put this good-smelling pine pillow on the rug beside him."

"Oh, boys," called Virginia from the hall down-stairs. "See what an enormous valentine pie Aunt Allison has made!"

Looking over the banisters, the boys saw that a table had been drawn into the middle of the wide reception-hall, and on it sat the largest pie that they had ever seen. It was in a bright new tin pan, and its daintily browned crust would have made them hungry even if their appetites had not been sharpened by the cold and exercise of the afternoon.

"What a queer place to serve pie," said Malcolm, in a disapproving undertone to his brother. "Why don't they have it in the dining-room? It looks mighty good, but somehow it doesn't seem proper to have it stuck out here in the hall. Mamma would never do such a thing."

"Aw, it's made of paper! She fooled us, sure, Malcolm," called back Keith, who had run on ahead to look. "It is only painted to look like a pie. But isn't it a splendid imitation?"

Virginia, pleased to have caught them so cleverly, showed them the ends of twenty-four pieces of narrow ribbon, peeping from under the delicately brown top crust. "The white ones are for the girls, and the red ones for the boys," she explained. "There is a valentine on the end of each one, and those on the red ribbons match the ones on the white. We'll all pull at once, and the ones who have valentines alike will go out to dinner together."

The guests came promptly. They had been invited for half-past six, and dinner was to be served soon after that time. The last to arrive was the Little Colonel. She came in charge of an old coloured woman, Mom Beck, who had been her mother's nurse as well as her own. The child was so hidden in her wraps when Mom Beck led her up-stairs, that no one could tell how she looked. The boys had been curious to see her, ever since they had heard so many tales of her mischievous pranks. A few minutes later, when she appeared in the parlours, there was a buzz of admiration. Maybe it was not so much for the soft light hair, the star-like beauty of her big dark eyes, or the delicate colour in her cheeks that made them as pink as a wild rose, as it was for the valentine costume she wore. It was of dainty white tulle, sprinkled with hundreds of tiny red velvet hearts, and there was a coronet of glittering rhinestones on her long fair hair.

"The Queen of Hearts," announced Aunt Allison, leading her forward. "You know 'she made some tarts, upon a summer day,' and now she shall open the valentine pie and see if it is as good as her Majesty's."

The big music-box in the hall began playing one of its liveliest waltzes, the children gathered around the great pie, and twenty-four little hands reached out to grasp the floating ends of ribbon.

"Pull!" cried the little Queen of Hearts. The paper crust flew off, and twenty-four yards of ribbon, each with a valentine attached, fluttered brightly through the air for an instant.

24

"Now match your verses," cried her Majesty again, opening her own to read what was in it. There was much laughing and peeping over shoulders, and tangling of white and scarlet ribbons, while the gay music-box played on.

In the midst of it Virginia beckoned to the Little Colonel. "Come up-stairs with me for a minute, Lloyd," she whispered, "and help me look for something. Aunt Allison has forgotten where she put the box of arrows that we are to use in the archery contest after dinner. There is the prettiest prize for the one who hits the red heart in the centre of the target."

"Oh, do you suppose you can hit it?" asked Lloyd, as she and Virginia slipped their arms around each other, and went skipping up the stairs.

"Yes, indeed!" answered Virginia. "I used to practise so much with my Indian bow and arrow out at the fort, that I could hit centre nearly every time. I am not going to shoot to-night. Aunt Allison thinks it wouldn't be fair."

When they reached the top of the stairs, Virginia went into her room to light a wax taper in one of the tall silver candlesticks on her dressing-table. "I think that Aunt Allison must have left those arrows in the blue room," she said, leading the way down the cross hall which went to the north wing. "She made the pie in there this morning, and all the other things were there. Nobody comes over in this part of the house much in winter, unless there happens to be a great deal of company."

The taper that Virginia carried was the only light in that part of the house. When she reached the door of the blue room she turned to Lloyd. "Hold the candle for me, please," she said, "while I look in the closet."

It was a pretty picture that the little "Queen of Hearts" made, as she stood in the doorway, with the tall silver candlestick held high in both hands. Her hair shone like gold in the candlelight, and her glittering crown flashed as if a circle of fairy fireflies had been caught in its soft meshes. Her dark eyes peered anxiously around the big shadowy room, lighted only by her flickering taper.

Down-stairs, Malcolm and Keith were almost quarrelling about her. It began by Malcolm taking his brother aside and offering to trade valentines with him.

"Why?" asked Keith, suspiciously.

"'Cause yours matches the Little Colonel's, and I want to take her out to dinner," admitted Malcolm. "She is the prettiest girl here."

"But I don't want to trade," answered Keith. "I want to take her myself."

"I'll give you the pick of any six stamps in my album if you will."

"Don't want your old stamps," declared Keith, stoutly. "I'd rather have the Little Colonel for my partner."

"I think you might trade," coaxed Malcolm. "It's mean not to when I'm the oldest. I'll give you that Chinese puzzle you've been wanting so long if you will." Keith shook his head.

Just then a terrific scream sounded in the upper hall, followed by another that made every one down-stairs turn pale with fright. Two voices were uttering piercing shrieks, one after another, so loud and frantic that even the servants in the back part of the house came running. Miss Allison, thinking of the candle she had told Virginia to light, and remembering the thin, white dress the child wore, instantly thought she must have set herself afire. She ran into the hall, so frightened that she was trembling from head to foot. Before she could reach the staircase, Virginia came flying down the steps, white as a little ghost, and her eyes wide with terror. Throwing herself into her aunt's outstretched arms, she began to sob out her story between great, trembling gasps.

"Oh, there's an awful, awful wild beast in the blue room, nearly as tall as the ceiling! It rose up and came after us out of the corner, and if I hadn't slammed the door just in time, it would have eaten us up. I'm sure it would! Oo-oo-oo! It was so awful!" she wailed.

"Why, Virginia," exclaimed her aunt, distressed to see her so terrified, "it must have been only a big shadow you saw. It isn't possible for a wild beast to be in the blue room you know. Where is Lloyd?"

"She's up heah, Miss Allison," called Mom Beck's voice. "She's so skeered, I'se pow'ful 'fraid she gwine to faint. They sut'nly is something in that room, honey, deed they is. I kin heah it movin' around now, switchin' he's tail an' growlin'!"

Malcolm and Keith, with guilty faces, went dashing up the stairs, and the whole party followed them at a respectful distance. When they opened the door the room looked very big and shadowy, and the bear, roused from its nap, was standing on its hind legs beside the high-posted bed. The huge figure was certainly enough to frighten any one coming upon it unexpectedly in the dark, and when Miss Allison saw it she drew Virginia's trembling hand into hers with a sympathetic clasp. Before she could ask any questions, the boys began an excited explanation. It was some time before they could make their story understood.

Their grandmother was horrified, and insisted on sending the animal away at once. "The idea of bringing such a dangerous creature into any one's house," she exclaimed, "and, above all, of shutting him up in a bedroom! We might have all been bitten, or hugged to death!"

"But, grandmother," begged Malcolm, "he isn't dangerous. Let me bring him into the light, and show you what a kind old pet he is."

There was a scattering to the other end of the hall as Malcolm came out, leading the bear, but the children gradually drew nearer as the great animal began its performances. Keith whistled and kept time with his feet in a funny little shuffling jig he had learned from Jonesy, and the bear obligingly went through all his tricks. He was used to being pulled out to perform whenever a crowd could be collected.

Virginia forgot her fear of him when he stood up and presented arms like a real soldier, and even went up and patted him when the show was over, joining with the boys in begging that he might be allowed to stay in the house until morning. Mrs. MacIntyre was determined to send a man down to the cabin at once to investigate. She had a horror of tramps. But the boys begged her to wait until daylight for Jonesy's sake.

"The man will beat him if he finds out that Jonesy warned us," pleaded Keith. He was so earnest that the tears stood in his big, trustful eyes.

"This is spoiling the party, mother," whispered Miss Allison, "and dinner is waiting. I'll be responsible for any harm that may be done if you will let the boys have their way this once."

There seemed no other way to settle it just then, so Bruin was allowed to go back to his rug in the blue room, and the door was securely locked.

Keith took Lloyd down to dinner, and his grandmother heard him apologising all the way down for having frightened her. The little Queen of Hearts listened smilingly, but her colour did not come back all evening, until after the archery contest. It was when Malcolm came up with the prize he had won, a tiny silver arrow, and pinned it in the knot of red ribbon on her shoulder.

"Will you keep it to remember me by?" he asked, bashfully.

"Of co'se!" she answered, with a smile that showed all her roguish dimples. "I'll keep it fo'evah and evah to remembah how neah I came to bein' eaten up by yo' bea'h."

"'WILL YOU KEEP IT TO REMEMBER ME BY?'"

"It seems too bad for such a beautiful party to come to an end," Sally Fairfax said when the last merry game was played, the last story told, and it was time to go home. "But there's one comfort," she added, gathering all her gay valentines together, "there needn't be any end to the remembering of it. I've had *such* a good time, Mrs. MacIntyre."

It was so late when the last carriage rolled down the avenue, bearing away the last smiling little guest, that the children were almost too sleepy to undress. It was not long until the last light was put out in every room, and a deep stillness settled over the entire house. One by one the lights went out in every home in the valley, and only the stars were left shining, in the cold wintry sky. No, there was one lamp that still burned. It was in the little cottage where old Professor Heinrich sat bowed over his books.

CHAPTER IV.

A FIRE AND A PLAN.

Some people said that old Johann Heinrich never slept, for no matter what hour of the night one passed his lonely little house, a lamp was always burning. He was a queer old German naturalist, living by himself in a cottage adjoining the MacIntyre place. He had been a professor in a large university until he grew too old to keep his position. Why he should have chosen Lloydsborough Valley as the place to settle for the remainder of his life, no one could tell.

He kept kimself away from his neighbours, and spent so much time roaming around the woods by himself that people called him queer. They did not know that he had written two big books about the birds and insects he loved so well, or that he could tell them facts more wonderful than fairy tales about these little wild creatures of the woodland.

To-night he had read later than usual, and his fire was nearly out. He was too poor to keep a servant, so when he found that the coal-hod was empty he had to go out to the kitchen to fill it himself. That is why he saw something that happened soon after midnight, while everybody else in the valley was sound asleep.

Over in the cabin by the spring-house where the boys had left the tramp and Jonesy, a puff of smoke went curling around the roof. Then a tongue of flame shot up through the cedars, and another and another until the sky was red with an angry glare. It lighted up the eastern window-panes of the servants' cottage, but the inmates, tired from the unusual serving of the evening before, slept on. It shone full across the window of Virginia's room, but she was dreaming of being chased by bears, and only turned uneasily in her sleep.

The old professor, on his way to the kitchen, noticed that it seemed strangely light outside. He shuffled to the door and looked out.

"Ach Himmel!" he exclaimed, excitedly. "Somebody vill shust in his bed be burnt, if old Johann does not haste make!"

Not waiting to close the door behind him, or even to catch up something to protect his old bald head from the intense cold of the winter night, he ran out across the garden. His shuffling feet, in their flapping old carpet slippers, forgot their rheumatism, and his shoulders dropped the weight of their seventy years. He ran like a boy across the meadow, through the gap in the fence, and down the hill to the cabin by the spring.

All one side of it was in flames. The fire was curling around the front door and bursting through the windows with fierce cracklings. Dashing frantically around to the back door, he threw himself against it, shouting to know if any one was within. A blinding rush of smoke was his only answer as he backed away from the overpowering heat, but something fell across the door-sill in a limp little heap. It was Jonesy.

Dragging the child to a safe distance from the burning building, he ran back, fearing that some one else might be in danger, but this time the flames met him at the door, and it was impossible to go in. His hoarse shouting roused the servants, but by the time they reached the cabin the roof had fallen in, and all danger of the fire spreading to other buildings was over.

While the professor was bending over Jonesy, trying to bring him back to consciousness, Miss Allison came running down the path. She had an eiderdown quilt wrapped around her over her dressing-gown. The shouts had awakened her, also, and she had slipped out as quietly as possible, not wishing to alarm her mother.

"How did it happen?" she demanded, breathlessly. "Is the child badly burned? Is any one else hurt? Is the tramp in the cabin?"

No one gave any answer to her rapid questions. The old professor shook his head, but did not look up. He was bending over Jonesy, trying to restore him to consciousness. He seemed to know the right things to do for him, and in a little while the child opened his eyes and looked around wonderingly. In a few minutes he was able to tell what he knew about the fire.

It was not much, only a horrible recollection of being awakened by a feeling that he was choking in the thick smoke that filled the room; of hearing the boss swear at him to be quick and follow him or he would be burned to death. Then there had been an awful moment of groping through the blinding, choking smoke, trying to find a way out. The man sprang to a window and made his escape, but as the outside air rushed in through the opening he left, it seemed to fan the smoke instantly into flame.

Jonesy had struck out at the wall of fire with his helpless little hands, and then, half-crazed by the scorching pain, dropped to the floor and crawled in the opposite direction, just as the professor burst open the door.

The sight of the poor little blistered face brought the tears to Miss Allison's eyes, and she called two of the coloured men, directing them to carry Jonesy to the house, and then go at once for a doctor. But the professor interfered, insisting that Jonesy should be taken to his house. He said that he knew how to prepare the cooling bandages that were needed, and that he would sit up all night to apply them. He could not sleep anyhow, he said, after such great excitement.

"But I feel responsible for him," urged Miss Allison. "Since it happened on our place, and my little nephews brought him here, it seems to me that we ought to have the care of him."

The professor waved her aside, lifting Jonesy's head as tenderly as a nurse could have done, and motioned the coloured men to lift him up.

"No, no, fraulein," he said. "I have had eggsperience. It is besser the poor leedle knabe go mit me!"

There was no opposing the old man's masterful way. Miss Allison stepped aside for them to pass, calling after him her willingness to do the nursing he had taken upon himself, and insisting that she would come early in the morning to help.

Unc' Henry was left to guard the ruins, lest some stray spark should be blown toward the other buildings. "Dis yere ole niggah wa'n't mistaken aftah all," he muttered. "Dee was somebody prowlin' 'roun' de premises yistiddy evenin'." Then he searched the ground, all around the cabin, for footprints in the snow. He found some tracks presently, and followed them over the meadow in the starlight, across the road, and down the railroad track several rods. There they suddenly disappeared. The tramp had evidently walked on the rail some distance. If Unc' Henry had gone quarter of a mile farther up the track, he would have found those same sliding imprints on every other crosstie, as if the man had taken long running leaps in his haste to get away.

Jonesy stoutly denied that the man had set fire to the cabin. "We nearly froze to death that night," he said, when questioned about it afterward, "and the boss piled on an awful big lot of wood just before he went to bed."

"Then what made him take to his heels so fast if he didn't?" some one asked.

"I don't know," answered Jonesy. "He said that luck was always against him, and maybe he thought nobody would believe him if he did say that he didn't do it."

Several days after that Malcolm found the tramp's picture in the *Courier-Journal*. He was a noted criminal who had escaped from a Northern penitentiary some two months before, and had been arrested by the Louisville police. There was no mistaking him. That big, ugly scar branded him on cheek and forehead like another Cain.

"And to think that that terrible man was harboured on my place!" exclaimed Mrs. MacIntyre when she heard of it. "And you boys were down there in the cabin with him for hours! Sat beside him and talked with him! What will your mother say? I feel as if you had been exposed to the smallpox, and I cannot be too thankful now that the boy who was with him was not brought here. He isn't a fit companion for you. Not that the poor little unfortunate is to blame. He cannot help being a child of the slums, and he must be put in an orphan asylum or a reform school at once. It is probably the only thing that can save him from growing up to be a criminal like the man who brought him here. I shall see what can be done about it, as soon as possible."

"A child of the slums!" Malcolm and Keith repeated the expression afterward, with only a vague idea of its meaning. It seemed to set poor Jonesy apart from themselves as something unclean,-- something that their happy, well-filled lives must not be allowed to touch.

Maybe if Jonesy had been an attractive child, with a sensitive mouth, and big, appealing eyes, he might have found his way more easily into people's hearts. But he was a lean, snub-nosed little fellow, with a freckled face and neglected hair. No one would ever find his cheek a tempting one to kiss, and no one would be moved, by any feeling save pity, to stoop and put affectionate arms around Jonesy. He was only a common little street gamin, as unlovely as he was unloved.

"What a blessing that there are such places as orphan asylums for children of that class," said Mrs. MacIntyre, after one of her visits to him. "I must make arrangements for him to be put into one as soon as he is able to be moved."

"I think he will be very loath to leave the old professor," answered Miss Allison. "He has been so good to the child, amusing him by the hour with his microscopes and collections of insects, telling him those delightful old German folk-lore tales, and putting him to sleep every night to the music of his violin. What a child-lover he is, and what a delightful old man in every way! I am glad we have discovered him."

"Yes," said Mrs. MacIntyre; "and when this little tramp is sent away, I want the children to go there often. I asked him if he could not teach them this spring, at least make a beginning with them in natural history, and he appeared much pleased. He is as poor as a church mouse, and would be very glad of the money."

"That reminds me," said Miss Allison, "he asked me if the boys could not come down to see Jonesy this afternoon, and bring the bear. He thought it would give the little fellow so much pleasure, and might help him to forget his suffering."

Mrs. MacIntyre hesitated. "I do not believe their mother would like it," she answered. "Sydney is careful enough about their associates, but Elise is doubly particular. You can imagine how much badness this child must know when you remember how he has been reared. He told me that his name is Jones Carter, and that he cannot remember ever having a father or a mother. I questioned him very closely this morning. He comes from the worst of the Chicago slums. He slept in the cellar of one of its poorest tenement houses, and lived in the gutters. He has a brother only a little older, who is a bootblack. On days when shines were plentiful they had something to eat, otherwise they starved or begged."

"Poor little lamb," murmured Miss Allison.

"It was by the brother's advice he came away with that tramp," continued Mrs. MacIntyre. "He had gotten possession of that trained bear in some way, and probably took a fancy to Jones because he could whistle and dance all sorts of jigs. He probably thought it would be a good thing to have a child with him to work on peoples' sympathies. They walked all the way from Chicago to Lloydsborough, Jones told me, excepting three days' journey they made in a wagon. They have been two months on the road, and showed the bear in the country places they passed through. They avoided the large towns."

"Think what a Christmas he must have had!" exclaimed Miss Allison.

"Christmas! I doubt if he ever heard the word. His speech is something shocking; nothing but the slang of the streets, and so ungrammatical that I could scarcely understand him at times. No, I am very sure that neither Sydney nor Elise would want the boys to be with him."

"But he is so little, mother, and so sick and pitiful looking," pleaded Miss Allison. "Surely he cannot know so very much badness or hurt the boys if they go down to cheer him up for a little while."

Notwithstanding Mrs. MacIntyre's fears, she consented to the boys visiting Jonesy that afternoon. She could not resist the professor's second appeal or the boys' own urging.

They took the bear with them, which Jonesy welcomed like a lost friend. They spent an interesting hour among the professor's collections, listening to his explanations in his funny broken English. Then they explored his cottage, much amused by his queer housekeeping, cracked nuts on the hearth, and roasted apples on a string in front of the fire.

Jonesy did not seem to be cheered up by the visit as much as the professor had expected. Presently the old man left the room and Keith sat down on the side of the bed.

"What makes you so still, Jonesy?" he asked. "You haven't said a word for the last half hour."

"I was thinking about Barney," he answered, keeping his face turned away. "Barney is my brother, you know."

"Yes, so grandmother said," answered Keith. "How big is he?"

"'Bout as big as yourn." There was a choke in Jonesy's voice now. "Seein' yourn put his arm across your shoulder and pullin' your head back by one ear and pinchin' you sort in fun like, made me think the way Barney uster do to me."

Keith did not know what to say, so there was a long, awkward pause.

"I'd never a-left him," said Jonesy, "but the boss said it 'ud only be a little while and we'd make so much money showin' the bear that I'd have a whole pile to take home. I could ride back on the cars and take a whole trunk full of nice things to Barney,--clothes, and candy, and a swell watch and chain, and a bustin' beauty of a bike. Now the bear's sold and the boss has run away, and I don't know how I can get back to Barney. Him an me's all each other's got, and I want to see him *so* bad."

The little fellow's lip quivered, and he put up one bandaged hand to wipe away the hot tears that would keep coming, in spite of his efforts not to make a baby of himself. There was something so pitiful in the gesture that Keith looked across at Malcolm and then patted the bedclothes with an affectionate little hand.

"Never mind, Jonesy," he said, "papa will be home in the spring and he'll send you back to Barney." But Jonesy never having known anything of fathers whose chief pleasure is in spending money to make little sons happy, was not comforted by that promise as much as Keith thought he ought to be.

"But I won't be here then," he sobbed. "They're goin' to put me in a 'sylum, and I can't get out for so long that maybe Barney will be dead before we ever find each other again."

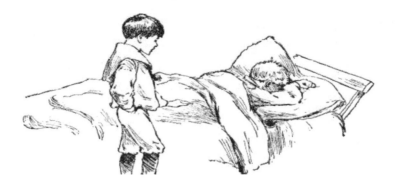

He was crying violently now.

"Who is going to put you in an asylum?" asked Malcolm, lifting an end of the pillow under which Jonesy's head had burrowed, to hide the grief that his eight-year-old manhood made him too proud to show.

"An old lady with white hair what comes here every day. The professor said he would keep me if he wasn't so old and hard up, and she said as how a 'sylum was the proper place for a child of the slums, and he said yes if they wasn't nobody to care for 'em. But I've got somebody!" he cried. "I've got Barney! Oh, *don't* let them shut me up somewhere so I can't never get back to Barney!"

"They don't shut you up when they send you to an asylum," said Malcolm. "The one near here is a lovely big house, with acres of green grass around it, and orchards and vine-yards, and they are ever so good to the children, and give them plenty to eat and wear, and send them to school."

"Barney wouldn't be there," sobbed Jonesy, diving under the pillow again. "I don't want nothing but him."

"Well, we'll see what we can do," said Malcolm, as he heard the professor coming back. "If we could only keep you here until spring, I am sure that papa would send you back all right. He's always helping people that get into trouble."

Jonesy took his little snub nose out of the pillow as the professor came in, and looked around defiantly as if ready to fight the first one who dared to hint that he had been crying. The boys took their leave soon after, leading the bear back to his new quarters in the carriage house, where they had made him a comfortable den. Then they walked slowly up to the house, their arms thrown across each other's shoulders.

"S'pose it was us," said Keith, after walking on a little way in silence. "S'pose that you and I were left of all the family, and didn't have any friends in the world, and I was to get separated from you and couldn't get back?"

"That would be tough luck, for sure," answered Malcolm.

"Don't you s'pose Jonesy feels as badly about it as we would?" asked Keith.

"Shouldn't be surprised," said Malcolm, beginning to whistle. Keith joined in, and keeping step to the tune, like two soldiers, they marched on into the house.

Virginia found them in the library, a little while later, sitting on the hearth-rug, tailor-fashion. They were still talking about Jonesy. They could think of nothing else but the loneliness of the little waif, and his pitiful appeal: "Oh, don't let them shut me up where I can't never get back to Barney."

"Why don't you write to your father?" asked Virginia, when they had told her the story of their visit.

"Oh, it is so hard to explain things in a letter," answered Malcolm, "and being off there, he'd say that grandmother and all the grown people certainly know best. But if he could see Jonesy,--how pitiful looking he is, and hear him crying to go back to his brother, I know he'd feel the way we do about it."

"I called the professor out in the hall, and told him so," said Keith, "and asked him if he couldn't adopt Jonesy, or something, until papa comes home. But he said that he is too poor. He has only a few dollars a month to live on. I didn't mind asking him. He smiled in that big, kind way he always does. He said Jonesy was lots of company, and he would like to keep him this summer, if he could afford it, and let him get well and strong out here in the country."

"Then he would keep him till Uncle Sydney comes, if somebody would pay his board?" asked Virginia.

"Yes," said Malcolm, "but that doesn't help matters much, for we children are the only ones who want him to stay, and our monthly allowances, all put together, wouldn't be enough."

"We might earn the money ourselves," suggested Virginia, after awhile, breaking a long silence.

"How?" demanded Malcolm. "Now, Ginger, you know, as well as I do, there is no way for us to earn anything this time of year. You can't pick fruit in the dead of winter, can you? or pull weeds, or rake leaves? What other way is there?"

"We might go to every house in the valley, and exhibit the bear," said Keith, "taking up a collection each time."

"Now you've made me think of it," cried Virginia, excitedly. "I've thought of a good way. We'll give Jonesy a benefit, like great singers have. The bear will be the star performer, and we'll all act, too, and sell the tickets, and have tableaux. I love to arrange tableaux. We were always having them out at the fort."

"I bid to show off the bear," cried Malcolm, entering into Virginia's plan at once. "May be I'll learn something to recite, too."

36

"I'll help print the tickets," said Keith, "and go around selling them, and be in anything you want me to be. How many tableaux are you going to have, Ginger?"

"I can't tell yet," she answered, but a moment after she cried out, her eyes shining with pleasure, "Oh, I've thought of a lovely one. We can have the Little Colonel and the bear for 'Beauty and the Beast.'"

Malcolm promptly turned a somersault on the rug, to express his approval, but came up with a grave face, saying, "I'll bet that grandmother will say we can't have it."

"Let's get Aunt Allison on our side," suggested Virginia. "She's up in her room now, painting a picture."

A little sigh of disappointment escaped Miss Allison's lips, as she heard the rush of feet on the stairs. This was the first time that she had touched her brushes since the children's coming, and she had hoped that this one afternoon would be free from interruption, when she heard them planning their afternoon's occupations at the lunch-table. They had come back before the little water-colour sketch she was making was quite finished.

There was no disappointment, however, in the bright face she turned toward them, and Virginia lost no time in beginning her story. She had been elected to tell it, but before it was done all three had had a part in the telling, and all three were waiting with wistful eyes for her answer.

"Well, what is it you want me to do?" she asked, finally.

"Oh, just be on our side!" they exclaimed, "and get grandmother to say yes. You see she doesn't feel about Jonesy the way we do. She is willing to pay a great deal of money to have him taken off and cared for, but she says she doesn't see how grandchildren of hers can be so interested in a little tramp that comes from nobody knows where, and who will probably end his days in a penitentiary."

Aunt Allison answered Malcolm's last remark a little sternly. "You must understand that it is only for your own good that she is opposed to Jonesy's staying," she said. "There is nobody in the valley so generous and kind to the poor as your grandmother." "Yes'm," said Virginia, meekly, "but you'll ask her, won't you please, auntie?"

Miss Allison smiled at her persistence. "Wait until I finish this," she said. "Then I'll go downstairs and put the matter before her, and report to you at dinner-time. Now are you satisfied?"

"Yes," they cried in chorus, "you're on our side. It's all right now!" With a series of hearty hugs that left her almost breathless, they hurried away.

When Miss Allison kept her promise she did not go to her mother with the children's story of Jonesy, to move her to pity. She told her simply what they wanted, and then said, "Mother, you know I have begun to teach the children the 'Vision of Sir Launfal.' Virginia has learned every word of it, and the boys will soon know all but the preludes. There will never be a better chance than this for them to learn the lesson:

"'Not what we give, but what we share,
 For the gift without the giver is bare.'

"This would be a real sharing of themselves, all their time and best energies, for they will have to work hard to get up such an entertainment as this. It isn't for Jonesy's sake I ask it, but for the children's own good."

The old lady looked thoughtfully into the fire a moment, and then said, "Maybe you are right, Allison. I do want to keep them unspotted from a knowledge of the world's evils, but I do not want to make them selfish. If this little beggar at the gate can teach them where to find the Holy Grail, through unselfish service to him, I do not want to stand in the way. Bless their little hearts, they may play Sir Launfal if they want to, and may they have as beautiful a vision as his!"

CHAPTER V.

JONESY'S BENEFIT.

The Jonesy Benefit grew like Jack's bean-stalk after Miss Allison took charge of it. There was less than a week in which to get ready, as the boys insisted on having it on the twenty-second of February, in honour of Washington's birthday; but in that short time the childish show which Ginger had proposed grew into an entertainment so beautiful and elaborate that the neighbourhood talked of it for weeks after.

Miss Allison spent one sleepless night, planning her campaign like a general, and next morning had an army of helpers at work. Before the day was over she sent a letter to an old school friend of hers in the city, Miss Eleanor Bond, who had been her most intimate companion all through her school-days, and who still spent a part of every summer with her.

"Dearest Nell," the letter said, "come out to-morrow on the first afternoon train, if you love me. The children are getting up an entertainment for charity, which shall be duly explained on your arrival. No time now. I am superintending a force of carpenters in the college hall, where the entertainment is to take place, have two seamstresses in the house hurrying up costumes, and am helping mother scour the country for pretty children to put in the tableaux.

"The house is like an ant-hill in commotion, there is so much scurrying around; but I know that is what you thoroughly enjoy. You shall have a finger in every pie if you will come out and help me to make this a never-to-be-forgotten occasion.

"I want to make the old days of chivalry live again for Virginia and Malcolm and Keith. I am going back to King Arthur's Court for the flower of knighthood at his round table. Come and read for us between tableaux as only you can do. Be the interpreter of 'Sir Launfal's Vision' and the 'Idylls of the King,' Give us the benefit of your talent for sweet charity's sake, if not for the sake of 'auld lang syne' and your devoted ALLISON."

"She'll be here," said Miss Allison, as she sealed the letter, nodding confidently to Mrs. Sherman, who had come over to help with Lloyd's costume. "You remember Nell Bond, do you not? She took the prize every year in elocution, and was always in demand at every entertainment. She is the most charming reader I ever heard, and as for story-telling--well, she's better than the 'Arabian Nights.' You must let the Little Colonel come over every evening while she is here."

Miss Bond arrived the next day, and her visit was a time of continual delight to the children. They followed her wherever she went, until Mrs. MacIntyre laughingly called her the 'Pied Piper of Hamelin,' and asked what she had done to bewitch them.

The first night they gathered around the library-table, all as busy as bees. Keith and the Little Colonel were cutting tinsel into various lengths for Virginia to tie into fringe for a gay banner. Malcolm was gilding some old spurs, Mrs. MacIntyre sat stringing yards of wax beads, that gleamed softly in the lamplight like great rope of pearls, and Mrs. Sherman was painting the posters, which were to be put up in the post-office and depot as advertisements of the Jonesy Benefit.

Miss Allison, who had been busy for hours with pasteboard and glue, tin-foil and scissors, held up the suit of mail which she had just finished.

"Isn't that fine!" cried Malcolm. "It looks exactly like some of the armour we saw in the Tower of London, doesn't it, Keith?"

"I've thought of a riddle!" exclaimed Virginia. "Why is Aunt Allison's head like Aladdin's lamp?"

"'Cause it's so bright?" ventured Malcolm.

"No; because she has only to rub it, and everything she thinks of appears. I don't see how it is possible to make so many beautiful things out of almost nothing."

Virginia looked admiringly around at all the pretty articles scattered over the room. A helmet with nodding white plumes lay on the piano. A queen's robe trailed its royal ermine beside it. A sword with a jewelled hilt shone on the mantel, and a dozen dazzling shields were ranged in various places on the low bookshelves.

It was easy, in the midst of such surroundings, for the children to imagine themselves back in the days of King Arthur and his court, while Miss Bond sat there telling them such beautiful tales of its fair ladies and noble knights. Indeed, before the day of the entertainment came around they even found themselves talking to each other in the quaint speech of that olden time.

When Malcolm accidentally ran against his grandmother in the hall, instead of his usual, "Oh, excuse me, grandmother," it was "Prithee grant me gracious pardon, fair dame. Not for a king's ransom would I have thus jostled thee in such unseemly haste!" And Ginger, instead of giving Keith a slap when he teasingly penned her up in a corner, to make her divide some nuts with him, said, in a most tragic way, "Unhand me, villain, or by my troth thou'lt rue this ruffian conduct sore!"

The library-table was strewn with books of old court life, and pictures of kings and queens whose costumes were to be copied in the tableaux. There was one book which Keith carried around with him until he had spelled out the whole beautiful tale. It was called "In Kings' Houses," and was the story of the little Duke of Gloster who was made a knight in his boyhood. And when Keith had read it himself, he took it down to the professor's, and read it all over again to Jonesy.

"THERE WAS ONE BOOK WHICH KEITH CARRIED AROUND WITH HIM."

"Think how grand he must have looked, Jonesy," cried Keith, "and I am to be dressed exactly like him when I am knighted in the tableau." Then he read the description again:

"'A suit of white velvet embroidered with seed pearls, and literally blazing with jewels,--even the buttons being great brilliants. From his shoulder hung a cloak of azure blue velvet, the colour of the order, richly wrought with gold; and around his neck he wore the magnificent collar and jewel of St. George and the Dragon, that was the personal gift of his Majesty, the king.'

"Think how splendid it must have been, Jonesy, when the procession came in to the music of trumpets and bugles and silver flutes and hautboys! Wouldn't you like to have seen the heralds marching by, two by two, in cloth of gold, with an escort of the queen's guard following? All of England's best and bravest were there, and they sat in the carven stalls in St. George's Chapel, with their gorgeous banners drooping over them. I saw that chapel, Jonesy, when we were in England, and I saw where the knights kept the 'vigil of arms' in the holy places, the night before they took their vows." He picked up the book and read again: "'Fasting and praying and lonely watching by night in the great abbey where there are so many dead folk.'

"Oh, don't you wish you could have lived in those days, Jonesy, and have been a knight?"

It was all Greek to Jonesy. The terms puzzled him, but he enjoyed Keith's description of the tournaments.

Several evenings after that, Keith went down to the cottage dressed in the beautiful velvet costume of white and blue, ablaze with rhinestones and glittering jewels. He had been wrapped in his Aunt Allison's golf cape, and, as he threw it off, Jonesy's eyes opened wider and wider with wonder.

"Hi! You look like a whole jeweller's window!" he cried, dazzled by the gorgeous sight. The professor lighted another lamp, and Keith turned slowly around, to be admired on every side like a pleased peacock.

"Of course it's all only imitation," he explained, "but it will look just as good as the real thing behind the footlights. But you ought to see the stage when it's fixed up to look like the Hall of the Shields, if you want to see glitter. It's be-*yu*-tiful! Like the one at Camelot, you know."

But Jonesy did not know, and Keith had to tell about that old castle at Camelot, as Miss Bond had told him. How that down the side of the long hall ran a treble range of shields,--

"And under every shield a knight was named,
 For such was Arthur's custom in his hall.
 When some good knight had done one noble deed
 His arms were carven only, but if twain
 His arms were blazoned also, but if none
 The shield was blank and bare, without a sign,
 Saving the name beneath."

Keith had been greatly interested in watching the carpenters fix the stage so that it could be made to look like the Hall of the Shields in a very few moments, when the time for that tableau should come. He knew where every glittering shield was to hang, and every banner and battle-axe.

"How do you suppose those knights felt," he said to Jonesy, "who saw their shields hanging there year after year, blank and bare, because they had never done even one noble deed? They must have been dreadfully ashamed when the king walked by and read their names underneath, and then looked up at the shields and saw nothing emblazoned on them or even carved. Seems to me that I would have done something to have made me worthy of that honour if I had *died* for it!"

Something,--it may have been the soft, rich colour of the jewel-broidered velvet the boy wore, or maybe the flush that rose to his cheeks at the thrill of such noble thoughts,--something had brought an unusual beauty into his face. As he stood there, with head held high, his dark eyes flashing, his face glowing, and in that princely dress of a bygone day, he looked every inch a nobleman. There was something so pure and sweet, too, in the expression of his upturned face that the light upon it seemed to touch it into an almost unearthly fairness.

The professor, who had been watching him with a tender smile on his rugged old face, drew the child toward him, and brushed the hair back on his forehead.

"Ach, liebchen," he said, in his queer broken speech, "thy shield will never be blank and bare. Already thou hast blazoned it with the beauty of a noble purpose, and like Galahad, thou too shalt find the Grail."

It was Keith's turn to be puzzled, but he did not like to ask for an explanation; there was something so solemn in the way the old man put his hand on his head as he spoke, almost as if he were bestowing a blessing. Besides, it was time to go to the rehearsal at the college. One of the servants had come to stay with Jonesy while the professor went over to practise on his violin. He was to play behind the scenes, a soft, low accompaniment to Miss Bond's reading.

By eight o'clock, the night of the Benefit, every seat in the house was full. "That's jolly for Jonesy," exclaimed Malcolm, peeping out from behind the curtain. "We counted up that ten cents a ticket would make enough, if they were all sold, to pay his board till papa comes home, and buy him all the new clothes he needs, too. Now every ticket is sold."

"Hurry up, Malcolm," called Keith. "We are first on the programme, and it is time to begin."

There was a great bustle behind the scenes for a few minutes, and then "Beauty and the Beast" was announced. When the Little Colonel came on the stage leading the great bear, such a cheering and clapping began that they both looked around, half frightened; but the boys followed immediately and the Little Colonel, dressed as a flower girl, danced out to meet Keith, who came in clicking his castanets in time to Malcolm's whistling. The bear was made to go through all his tricks and his soldier drill.

43

The children in the audience stood on tiptoe in their eagerness to see the great animal perform, and were so wild in their applause that the boys begged to be allowed to take it in front of the curtain every time during the evening when there was a long pause while some tableau was being prepared.

Over the rustle of fluttering programmes and the hum of conversation that followed the first number, there fell presently the soft, sweet notes of the professor's violin, and Miss Bond's musical voice began the story of the Vision of Sir Launfal.

"My golden spurs now bring to me,
 And bring to me my richest mail,
 For to-morrow I go over land and sea
 In search of the Holy Grail."

Here the curtains were drawn apart to show Malcolm seated on his pony as Sir Launfal, "in his gilded mail that flamed so bright." It was really a beautiful picture he made, and his grandmother, leaning forward, her face beaming with pride at the boy's noble bearing, compared him with Arthur himself, "with lance in rest, from spur to plume a star of tournament,"

The next tableau showed him spurning the leper at his gate, and turning away in disgust from the beggar who "seemed the one blot on the summer morn." How Miss Bond's voice rang out when "the leper raised not the gold from the dust."

"Better to me the poor man's crust.
 That is no true alms which the hand can hold.
 He gives nothing but worthless gold
 Who gives from a sense of duty."

In the next tableau it was "as an old bent man, worn-out and frail," that Sir Launfal came back from his weary pilgrimage. He had not found the Holy Grail, but through his own sufferings he had learned pity for all pain and poverty. Once more he stood beside the leper at his castle gate, but this time he stooped to share with him his crust and wooden bowl of water.

Then it happened on the stage just as was told in the poem.

A light shone round about the place, and the crouching leper stood up. The old ragged mantle dropped off, and there in a long garment almost dazzling in its whiteness, stood a figure--

"Shining and tall, and fair, and straight
 As the pillar that stood by the Beautiful gate."

They could not see the face, it was turned aside; but the golden hair was like a glory, and the uplifted arms held something high in air that gleamed like a burnished star, as all the lights in the room were turned full upon it, for a little space. It was a golden cup. Then the voice again:

"In many climes without avail
 Thou hast spent thy life for the Holy Grail.

Behold it is here--this cup, which thou
Didst fill at the streamlet for me but now.
The holy supper is kept indeed
In whatso we share with another's need."

It was an old story to most of the audience, worn threadbare by many readings, but with these living illustrations, and Miss Bond's wonderful way of telling it, a new meaning crept into the well-known lines, that thrilled every listener.

"Could you understand that, Teddy?" asked old Judge Fairfax, patting his little grandson on the head.

"Course!" exclaimed seven-year-old Ted, who had followed his sister Sally to every rehearsal.

"When you give money to people just to get rid of 'em, and because you feel you'd ought to, it doesn't count for anything. But if you divide something you've got, and would like to keep it all yourself, because you love to, and are sorry for 'em, then it counts a pile. Sir Launfal would have popped Jonesy into a 'sylum when he first started out to find that gold cup, but when he came back he'd 'a' worked like a horse getting up a benefit for him, and would have divided his own home with him, if he hadn't been living at his grandmother's, and couldn't."

An amused smile went around that part of the audience which overheard Ted's shrilly given explanation.

Pictures from the "Idylls of the King" followed in rapid succession, and then came the prettiest of all, being the one in which Keith was made a knight. Virginia as queen, her short black hair covered by a powdered wig, and a long court-train sweeping behind her, stood touching his shoulder with the jewel-hilted sword, as he knelt at her feet. Lloyd and Sally Fairfax, Julia Ferris, and a dozen other pretty girls of the neighbourhood, helped to fill out the gay court scene, while all the boys that could be persuaded to take part were dressed up for heralds, guardsmen, pages, and knights. That tableau had to be shown four times, and then the audience kept on applauding as if they never intended to stop.

The last one in this series of tableaux was the Hall of the Shields, as Keith had described it to Jonesy. A whole row of dazzling shields hung across the back of the stage, emblazoned with the arms of all the old knights whose names have come down to us in song or story. Then for the first time that evening Miss Bond came out on the stage where she could be seen, and told the story of the death of King Arthur, and the passing away of the order of the Round Table. She told it so well that little Ted Fairfax listened with his mouth open, seeming to see the great arm that rose out of the water to take back the king's sword into the sea, from which it had been given him. An arm like a giant's, "clothed in white samite, mystic, wonderful, that caught the sword by the hilt, flourished it three times, and drew it under the mere."

"True, 'the old order changeth,'" said Miss Bond, "but knighthood has *not* passed away. The flower of chivalry has blossomed anew in this new world, and America, too, has her Hall of the Shields."

Just a moment the curtains were drawn together, and then were widely parted again, as a chorus of voices rang out with the words:

"Hail, Columbia, happy land;
 Hail, ye heroes, heaven-born band!"

In that moment, on every shield had been hung the pictured face of some well-known man who had helped to make his country a power among the nations; presidents, patriots, philanthropists, statesmen, inventors, and poets,--there they were, from army and navy, city and farm, college halls and humble cabins,--a long, long line, and the first was Washington, and the last was the "Hero of Manila."

Cheer after cheer went up, and it might have been well to have ended the programme there, but to satisfy the military-loving little Ginger, one more was added.

"There ought to be a Goddess of Liberty in it," she insisted, "because it is Washington's birthday; and if we had been doing it by ourselves we were going to have something in it about Cuba, on papa's account."

So when the curtain rose the last time, it was on Sally Fairfax as a gorgeous Goddess of Liberty, conferring knighthood on two boys who stood for the Army and Navy, while a little dark-eyed girl knelt at their feet as Cuba, the distressed maiden whom their chivalry had rescued.

It was late when the performance closed; later still when the children reached home that night, for Mrs. MacIntyre had determined to have a flash-light picture taken of them, and they had to wait until the photographer could send home for his camera.

After they reached the house they could hardly be persuaded to undress. Virginia trailed up and down the halls in her royal robes, Malcolm clanked around in his suit of mail and plumed helmet, and Keith stood before a mirror, admiring the handsome little figure it showed him.

"I hate to take it off," he said, fingering the dazzling collar, ablaze with jewels. "I'd like to be a knight always, and wear a sword and spurs every day."

"So would I," said Malcolm, beginning to yawn sleepily. "I wish that Jonesy had been well enough to go to-night. Isn't it splendid that the Benefit turned out so well? Aunt Allison says there is plenty of money now to get Jonesy's clothes and pay his board till papa comes, and send him back to Barney, too, if papa thinks best and hasn't any better plan."

"I wish there'd been enough money to buy a nice little home out here in the country for him and Barney. Wouldn't it have been lovely if there had a-been?" cried Keith.

"Well, I should say!" answered Malcolm. "Maybe we can have another benefit some day and make enough for that."

With this pleasant prospect before them, they laid aside their knightly garments, hoping to put them on again soon in Jonesy's behalf, and talked about the home that might be his some day, until they fell asleep.

The flash-light pictures of the three children were all that the fondest grandmother could wish. As soon as they came, Keith carried his away to his room to admire in private. "It is so pretty that it doesn't seem it can be me," he said, propping it up on the desk before him. "I wish that I could look that way always."

The next time that Miss Allison went into the room she found that Keith had written under it in his round, boyish hand, a quotation that had taken his fancy the first time he heard it. It was in one of Miss Bond's stories, and he repeated it until he learned it: "*Live pure, speak truth, right the wrong, follow the king; else wherefore born?*"

She asked him about it at bedtime. "Why, that's our motto," he explained. "Malcolm has it written under his, too. We've made up our minds to be a sort of knight, just as near the real thing as we can, you know, and that is what knights have to do: live pure, and speak truth, and right the wrong. We've always tried to do the first two, so that won't be so hard. It's righting the wrong that will be the tough job, but we have done it a little teenty, weenty bit for Jonesy, don't you think, auntie? It was all wrong that he should have such a hard time and be sent to an asylum away from Barney, when we have you all and everything nice. Malcolm and I have been talking it over. If we could do something to keep him from growing up into a tramp like that awful man that brought him here, wouldn't that be as good a deed as some that the real knights did? Wouldn't that be serving our country, too, Aunt Allison, just a little speck?" He asked the question anxiously. Malcolm said nothing, but also waited with a wistful look for her answer.

"My dear little Sir Galahads," she said, bending over to give each of the boys a good-night kiss, "you will be 'really truly' knights if you can live up to the motto you have chosen. Heaven help you to be always as worthy of that title as you are to-night!"

Keith held her a moment, with both arms around her neck. "What does that mean, auntie?" he asked. "That is what the professor said, too,--Galahad."

"It is too late to explain to you to-night," she said, "but I will tell you sometime soon, dear."

It was several days before she reminded them of that promise. Then she called them into her room and told them the story of Sir Galahad, the maiden knight, whose "strength was as the strength of ten because his heart was pure." Then from a little morocco case, lined with purple velvet, she took two pins that she had bought in the city that morning. Each was a little white enamel flower with a tiny diamond in the centre, like a drop of dew.

"You can't wear armour in these days," she said, as she fastened one on the lapel of each boy's coat, "but this shall be the badge of your knighthood,--'wearing the white flower of a blameless life.' The little pins will help you to remember, maybe, and will remind you that you are pledged to right the wrong wherever you find it, in little things as well as great."

It was a very earnest talk that followed. The boys came out from her room afterward, wearing the tiny white pins, and with a sweet seriousness in their faces. A noble purpose had been born in their hearts; but alas for chivalry! the first thing they did was to taunt Virginia with the fact that she could never be a knight because she was only a girl.

"I don't care," retorted Ginger, quickly. "I can be a--a--*patriot*, anyhow, and that's lots better."

The boys laughed, and she flushed angrily.

"They ought to mean the same thing exactly in this day of the world," said Miss Allison, coming up in time to hear the dispute that followed. "Virginia, you shall have a badge, too. Run into my room and bring me that little jewelled flag on my cushion."

"I think that this is the very prettiest piece of jewelry you have," exclaimed Virginia, coming back with the pin. It was a little flag whose red, white, and blue was made of tiny settings of garnets, sapphires, and diamonds.

"You think that, because it is in the shape of a flag," said Miss Allison, with an amused smile. "Well, it shall be yours. See how well it can remind you of the boys' knightly motto. There is the white for the first part, the 'live pure,' and the 'true blue' for the 'speak truth,' and then the red,--surely no soldier's little daughter needs to be told what that stands for, when her own brave father has spilled part of his good red life-blood to 'right the wrong' on the field of battle."

"Oh, Aunt Allison!" was all that Virginia could gasp in her delight as she clasped the precious pin tightly in her hand. "Is it mine? For my very own?"

"For your very own, dear," was the answer.

"Oh, I'm so glad!" cried Virginia, thanking her with a kiss. "I'd a thousand times rather have it than one like the boys'. It means so much more!"

CHAPTER VI.

THE LITTLE COLONEL'S TWO RESCUES.

Early in March, when the crocuses were beginning to bud under the dining-room windows, there came one of those rare spring days that seem to carry the warmth of summer in its sunshine.

"Exactly the kind of a day for a picnic," Virginia had said that morning, and when her grandmother objected, saying that the ground was still too damp, she suggested having it in the hay-barn. The boys piled the hay that was left from the winter's supply up on one side of the great airy room, set wide the big double doors, and swept it clean.

"It is clean enough now for even grandmother to eat in," said Virginia, as she spread a cloth on the table Unc' Henry had carried out for them. "It's good enough for a queen. Oh, I'll tell you what let's do. Let's play that Malcolm and I are a wicked king and queen and Lloyd is a 'fair ladye' that we have shut up in a dungeon. This will be a banquet, and while we are eating Keith can be the knight who comes to her rescue and carries her off on his pony."

"That's all right," consented Keith, "except the eating part. How can we get our share of the picnic?"

"We'll save it for you," answered Virginia, "and you can eat it afterward."

"Save enough for Jonesy, too," said Keith. "He shall be my page and help me rescue her. I'll go and ask him now."

The month had made a great change in Jonesy. With plenty to eat, his thin little snub-nosed face grew plump and bright. There was a good-humoured twinkle in his sharp eyes, and being quick as a monkey at imitating the movements of those around him, Mrs. MacIntyre found nothing to criticise in his manners when Malcolm and Keith brought him into the house. Their pride in him was something amusing, and seeing that, after all, he was an inoffensive little fellow, she made no more objections to their playing with him.

By the time Keith was back again with Jonesy, the other guests had arrived, and the Little Colonel had been lowered into a deep feed-bin, in lieu of a dungeon. The banquet began in great state, but in a few moments was interrupted by a fearful shrieking from the depths of the bin. The fair ladye protested that she would not stay in her dungeon.

"There's nasty big spidahs down heah!" she called. "Ow! One is crawlin' on my neck now, and my face is all tangled up in cobwebs! Get me out! Get me out! Quick, Gingah!"

The king sprang up to go to her rescue, but was promptly motioned to his seat again by a warning shake of the other crowned head.

"Why, of course! There's always spiders in dungeons," called the wicked queen, coolly helping herself to another piece of chicken. "Besides, you should say 'your Majesty' when you are talking to me."

"But there's a mouse in heah, too," she called back, in distress. "Oo! Oo! It ran ovah my feet. If you don't make them take me out of heah, Gingah Dudley, I'll do something *awful* to you! Murdah! Murdah!" she yelled, pounding on the sides of the bin with both her fists, and stamping her little foot in a furious rage.

"THE LITTLE COLONEL HAD BEEN LOWERED INTO A DEEP FEED-BIN."

Seeing that Lloyd was really terrified, and fearing that her screams would bring some one from the house, the royal couple and their guests sprang to the rescue, nearly upsetting the banquet as they did so. The game would have been broken up then, when she was lifted out from the feed-bin, red and angry, if it had not been for the king's great tact. He brushed the cobwebs from her face and hair, and even got down on his royal knees to ask her pardon.

His polite coaxing finally had its effect on the little lady, and he persuaded her to climb a ladder into a loft just above them. Here on a pile of clean hay, beside an open window that looked

51

across a peaceful meadow, her anger cooled. Towers were far more comfortable than dungeons, in her opinion, and when Malcolm came up the ladder with a plateful of the choicest morsels of the feast, she began to enjoy her part of the play. Jonesy was sent to inform his knight of the change from dungeon to tower, and the banquet went merrily on.

He found Keith waiting below the barn, with his pony tied to a fence. On the other side of the fence lay the railroad track, which skirted the back of Mrs. MacIntyre's place for over half a mile.

"Do you see that hand-car?" asked Keith, pointing with his riding-whip to one on the track. "The section boss let Malcolm and me ride up and down on it all afternoon one day this winter. Some workman left it on the switch while ago, and while you were up at the barn I got two darkeys to move it for me. They didn't want to at first, but I knew that there'd be no train along for an hour, and told 'em so, and they finally did it for a dime apiece. As soon as I rescue Lloyd I'll dash down here on my pony with her behind me. Then we'll slip through the fence and get on the hand-car, and be out of sight around the curve before the rest get here. They won't know where on earth we've gone, and it will be the best joke on them. It's down grade all the way to the section-house, so I can push it easily enough by myself, but I'll need your help coming back, maybe. S'pose you cut across lots to the section-house as soon as I start to the barn, and meet me there. It isn't half as far that way, so you'll get there as soon as we do."

"All right," said Jonesy. "I'm your kid."

"You should say, "'Tis well, Sir Knight, I fly to do thy bidding,'" prompted Keith.

Jonesy grinned. He could not enter into the spirit of the play as the others did. "Aw, I'll be on time," he said; then, as Keith untied his pony, started on a run across the fields.

The Lady Lloyd had not finished her repast when her rescuer appeared, but she put the plate down on the hay to await her return, and obediently climbed down the ladder he placed for her. They reached the fence before the banqueters knew that she had escaped. Flinging the pony's bridle over a fence-post, when they reached the edge of the field, the brave knight crawled through the fence and pulled Lloyd after him, tearing her dress, much to that dainty little lady's extreme disgust.

By the time the king and his guard were mounted in pursuit, on the other pony which stood in waiting, the runaways were in the hand-car. It moved slowly at first, although Keith was strong for his age, and his hardy little muscles were untiring.

"Isn't it lovely?" cried Lloyd, as they moved faster and faster and swept around the curve. "I wish we could go all the way to Louisville on this." The warm March wind fanned her pink cheeks, and blew her soft light hair into her eyes.

Jonesy was waiting at the section-house, and waved his cap as they passed. "We're going on, around the next bend," shouted Keith, as they passed him. "Whoop-la! this is fine, and not a bit hard to work!"

"What will the wicked queen think when she can't find us?" asked Lloyd, laughing happily, as they sped on down the track.

"She'll think that I am a magician and have spirited you away," said Keith.

"Then if you are a magician you ought to change her into a nasty black spidah, to pay her back fo' shuttin' me up with them!" Lloyd was delighted with this new play. For the time it seemed as if she really were escaping from a castle prison. Faster and faster they went. Jonesy, who had followed them to the second curve, stood watching them with wistful eyes, wishing he could be with them. They passed the depot, and then the hand-car seemed to grow smaller and smaller as it rolled away, until it was only a moving speck in the distance. Then he turned and walked back to the section-house.

"I s'pect we've gone about far enough," said Keith, after awhile. "We'd better turn around now and go back, or the picnic will all be over before we get our share. Let's wait here a minute till I rest my arms, and then we'll start."

The place where they had stopped was the loneliest part of the track that could be found in miles, on either side. It was in the midst of a thick beech woods, and the twitter of a bird, now and then, was the only sound in all the deep stillness.

"What lovely green moss on that bank!" cried the Little Colonel. "Wouldn't it make a beautiful carpet for our playhouse down by the old mill?"

"I'll get you some," said Keith, gallantly springing from the car and clambering up the bank. Taking out his knife, he began to cut great squares of the velvety green moss, and pile it up to carry back to the hand-car.

Meanwhile Jonesy waited at the section-house, digging his heels into the cinders that lined the track, and looking impatiently down the road. Presently the section boss came limping along painfully, and sat down on the bank in the warm spring sunshine. He had dropped a piece of heavy machinery on his foot, the week before, and was only able to hobble short distances.

Everybody in the Valley was interested in Jonesy since the fire and the Benefit had made him so well known, and the man was glad of this opportunity to satisfy his curiosity about the boy. Jonesy, with all the fearlessness of a little street gamin brought up in a big city, answered him fearlessly, even saucily at times, much to the man's amusement.

"So you want to get a job around here, do you?" said the man, presently, with a grin. "Maybe I can give you one. Know anything about railroadin'?"

"Heaps," answered Jonesy. "Well, I'd ought to, seem' as I've lived next door to the engine yards all my life, and spent my time dodgin' the cop on watch there, when I was tryin' to steal rides on freight-cars and such."

"Is that what you're hangin' around here now for?" asked the man, with a good-natured twinkle in his eyes.

"Nope! I'm waiting for that MacIntyre kid to come back this way. He went down the track a bit ago on a hand-car, playing rescue a princess with one of the girls at the picnic,"

The section boss sprang up with an exclamation of alarm. "How far's he gone?" he asked. "There's a special due to pass here in a few minutes."

Even while he spoke there sounded far away in the distance, so far that it was like only a faint echo, the whistle of an approaching locomotive. The man hobbled down the track a yard or so and stopped. "What do you suppose they'll do?" he asked. "There are so many bends in this road, the train may come right on to 'em before the engineer sees 'em. S'pose they'll jump off, or turn and try to come back?"

Jonesy glanced around wildly a second, and then sprang forward toward the man.

"Give me the switch-key!" he cried, in a high voice, shrill with excitement. "You can't run, but I can. Give me the switch-key!" Perplexed by the sudden turn of affairs and the little fellow's commanding tone, the man took the key from his pocket. He realised his own helplessness to do anything, and there was something in Jonesy's manner that inspired confidence. He felt that the child's quick wit had grasped the situation and formed some sensible plan of action.

Again the whistle sounded in the distance, and, snatching the key, Jonesy was off down the track like an arrow. The section boss, leaning heavily on his cane, limped after him as fast as he could.

Keith and the Little Colonel, having gathered the moss and started back home, were rolling leisurely along, still talking of magicians and their ilk.

"What if we should meet a dragon?" cried the Little Colonel. "A dragon with a scaly green tail, and red eyes and a fiery tongue. What would you do then?"

54

"I'd say, 'What! Ho! Thou monster!' and cleave him in twain with my good broadsword, and when he saw its shining blade smite through the air he'd just curl up and die."

Keith looked back to smile at the bright laughing face beside him. Then he caught sight of something over his shoulder that made him pause. "Oh, look!" he cried, pointing over the tree-tops behind them. A little puff of smoke, rising up in the distance, trailed along the sky like a long banner. At the same instant, out of the smoke, sounded the whistle of an approaching engine. The track behind them had so many turns, he could not judge of their distance from it, and for an instant he stopped working the handle bar up and down, too thoroughly frightened to know what to do. An older child might have acted differently; might have jumped from the hand-car and left it to be run into by the approaching train, or have hurried back around the bend to flag the engine. But Keith had only one idea left: that was to keep ahead of the train as long as possible. It seemed so far away he thought they could surely reach the depot before it caught up with them, and his sturdy little arms bent to the task.

For a moment there was a real pleasure in the exertion. He felt with an excited thrill that he was really running away with the Little Colonel, and rescuing her from a pursuing danger. Suddenly the whistle sounded again, and this time it seemed so close behind them that the Little Colonel gave a terrified glance over her shoulder and then screamed at the sight of the great snorting monster, breathing out fire and smoke, worse than any scaly-tailed dragon that she had ever imagined. It was far down the track but they could hear its terrible rumble as it rushed over a trestle, and the singing of the wires overhead.

Keith was straining every muscle now, but it was like running in a nightmare. His arms moved up and down at a furious speed, but it seemed to him that the hand-car was glued to one spot. It seemed, too, that it had been hours since they first discovered that the engine was after them, and he felt that he would soon be too exhausted to move another stroke. Would the depot never never come in sight?

Just then they shot around the curve and caught sight of Jonesy at the depot switch, wildly beckoning with his cap and shouting for them to come on. At that sight, with one supreme effort Keith put his fast-failing strength to the test, and sent the hand-car rolling forward faster than ever. It shot past the switch that Jonesy had unlocked and off to the side-track, just as the train bore down upon them around the last bend.

There was barely time for Jonesy to set the switch again before it thundered on along the main track past the little depot. Being a special, it did not stop. As it went shrieking by, the engineer cast a curious glance at a hand-car on the side-track. A little girl sat on it, a pretty golden-haired child with dark eyes big with fright, and her face as white as her dress. He wondered what was the matter.

For a moment after the shrieking train whizzed by everything seemed deathly still. Keith sat leaning against the embankment, white and limp from exhaustion and the excitement of his close escape. Jonesy was panting and wiping the perspiration from his red face, for he had run like a deer to reach the switch in time.

"I couldn't have held out a minute longer," said Keith, presently. "My arms felt like they had gone to sleep, and I was just ready to give up when I caught sight of you. That seemed to give me strength to go on, when I saw what you were at and that it would only be a little farther to go before we would be safe. Plow did you happen to be at the switch, and know how to set it?"

"Hain't lived all my life around engine yards fer nothin'," answered Jonesy. "Why didn't you jump off and flag the train?"

"I was so taken by surprise I didn't think of that," answered Keith. "The only thing I knew was that we had to keep ahead of it as long as possible. You've saved my life, Jones Carter, and I'll never forget it, no matter what comes,"

"I've been rescued twice to-day," said the Little Colonel, taking a deep breath as she began to recover from her fright. "Jonesy ought to be a knight, too."

"That's so!" exclaimed Keith, springing to his feet. "Come on and let's go back to the barn. We'll tell our adventures, and then we'll go through the ceremony of making Jonesy a Sir Something or other. He's certainly won his spurs."

"Goin' back on the hand-car?" asked Jonesy.

"Not much," answered Keith, with a sickly sort of smile. "Somehow such fast travelling doesn't seem to agree with a fellow. Walking is good enough for me."

"Me too!" cried the Little Colonel, tying on her white sunbonnet. "But the first part of it was lovely,--just like flyin'."

Jonesy ran back to give the man his key, and was kept answering questions so long that he did not catch up with the other children until they were in sight of the barn.

"After all," said Keith, as the three trudged along together, "maybe we'd better not tell how near we came to being run over. Grandmother and Aunt Allison would be dreadfully worried if they should hear of it. They are always worrying for fear something will happen to us."

"Mothah would be *wild*" exclaimed the Little Colonel, "if she knew I had been in any dangah. Maybe she wouldn't let me out of her sight again to play all summah."

"Then let's don't tell for a long, long time," proposed Keith. "It'll be our secret, just for us three."

"All right," the others agreed. They dropped the subject then, for the barn was just ahead of them, and the gay picnickers came running out, demanding to know where they had been so long.

The Little Colonel often spoke of her experience afterward to the two boys, however, and in Keith's day-dreams a home for Jonesy began to crowd out all other hopes and plans.

CHAPTER VII.

A GAME OF INDIAN.

Keith was stiff for a week after his race on the hand-car, but did his groaning in private. He knew what a commotion would be raised if the matter came to his grandmother's ears. She had lived all winter in constant dread of accidents. Malcolm had been carried home twice in an unconscious state, once from having been thrown from his bicycle, and once from falling through a trap-door in the barn. Keith had broken through the ice on the pond, sprained his wrist while coasting, and walked in half a dozen times with the blood streaming from some wound on his head or face.

Virginia had never been hurt, but her hair-breadth escapes would have filled a volume. An amusing one was the time she lassoed a young calf, Indian fashion, to show the boys how it should be done. Its angry mother was in the next lot, but Virginia felt perfectly safe as she swung her lariat and dragged the bleating calf around the barn-yard. She did not stop to consider that if a cow with lofty ambitions had once jumped over the moon, one which saw its calf in danger might easily leap a low hedge. Malcolm's warning shout came just in time to save her from being gored by the angry animal, who charged at her with lowered horns. She sprang up the ladder leading to the corn-crib window, where she was safe, but she had to hang there until Unc' Henry could be called to the rescue.

It was with many misgivings that Mrs. MacIntyre and Miss Allison started to the city one morning in April. It was the first time since the children's coming that they had both gone away at once, and nothing but urgent business would have made them consent to go.

The children promised at least a dozen things. They would keep away from the barn, the live stock, the railroad, the ponds, and the cisterns. They would not ride their wheels, climb trees, nor go off the MacIntyre premises, and they would keep a sharp lookout for snakes and poison ivy, in case they went into the woods for wild flowers.

VIRGINIA AND THE CALF.

"Seems to me there's mighty little left that a fellow can do," said Keith, when the long list was completed.

"Oh, the time will soon pass," said his grandmother, who was preparing to take the eleven o'clock train. "It will soon be lunch-time. Then this is the day for you each to write your weekly letters to your mother, and it is so pretty in the woods now that I am sure you will enjoy looking for violets."

Time did pass quickly, as their grandmother had said it would, until the middle of the afternoon. Then Virginia began to wish for something more amusing than the quiet guessing games they had been playing in the library. The boys each picked up a book, and she strolled off up-stairs, in search of a livelier occupation.

In a few minutes she came down, looking like a second Pocahontas in her Indian suit, with her bow and arrows slung over her shoulder.

"I am going down to the woods to practise shooting," she announced, as she stopped to look in at the door.

"Oh, wait just a minute!" begged Malcolm, throwing down his book. "Let's all play Indian this afternoon. We'll rig up, too, and build a wigwam down by the spring rock, and make a fire,-- grandmother didn't say we couldn't make a fire; that's about the only thing she forgot to tell us not to do."

"You can come on when you get ready," answered Virginia. "I'm going now, because it is getting late, but you'll find me near the spring when you come. Just yell."

The boys could not hope to rival Virginia's Indian costume, but no wilder-looking little savages ever uttered a war-whoop than the two which presently dashed into the still April woods.

Malcolm had ripped some variegated fringe from a table-cover to pin down the sides of his leather leggins. He had borrowed a Roman blanket from Aunt Allison's couch to pin around his shoulders, and emptied several tubes of her most expensive paints to streak his face with hideous stripes and daubs. A row of feathers from the dust-brush was fastened around his forehead by a broad band, and a hatchet from the woodshed provided him with a tomahawk.

Keith had no time to arrange feathers. He had taken off his flannels in order to put on an old striped bathing-suit, which he had found in the attic and stored away, intending to use it for swimming in the pond when the weather should grow warm enough. It had no sleeves, and the short trousers had shrunk until they did not half-way reach his knees. Its red and white stripes had faded and the colour run until the whole was a dingy "crushed strawberry" shade. As Malcolm had emptied all the tubes of red paint in his Aunt Allison's box, Keith had to content himself with some other colour. He chose the different shades of green, squeezing the paint out on his plump little legs and arms, and rubbing it around with his fore finger until he was encircled with as many stripes as a zebra. Although the day was warm for the early part of April, the sudden change from his customary clothes and spring flannels to nothing but the airy bathing suit and war-paint made him a trifle chilly; so he completed his costume by putting on a pair of scarlet bedroom slippers, edged with dark fur.

With the dropping of their civilised clothing, the boys seemed to have dropped all recollections of their professed knighthood, and acted like the little savages they looked.

"We're going to shoot with your things awhile, Ginger," shouted Keith, coming suddenly upon her with a whoop, and snatching her bow out of her hands. "You are the squaw, so you have to do all the work. Get down there now behind that rock and make a fire, while we go out and kill a deer. You must build a wigwam, too, by the time we get back. Hear me? I'm a big chief! 'I am Famine--Buckadawin!' and I'll make a living skeleton of you if you don't hustle."

Virginia was furious. "I'll not be a squaw!" she cried. "And I'll not build a fire or do anything else if you talk so rudely. If you don't give me back my bow and let me be a chief, too, I'll--I'll get even with you, sir, in a way you won't like. I have short hair, and my clothes are more Indian than yours, and I can shoot better than either of you, anyhow! So there! Give me my bow."

"What will you do if I won't?" said Keith, teasingly, holding it behind him.

"I'll go up to the barn and get a rope, and lasso you like I did that calf, and drag you all over the place!" cried Virginia, her eyes shining with fierce determination.

59

"She means it, Keith," said Malcolm. "She'll do it sure, if you don't stop teasing. Oh, give it to her and come along, or it will be dark before we begin to play."

Matters went on more smoothly after Malcolm's efforts at peacemaking, and when it was decided that Ginger could be a brave, too, instead of a squaw, they were soon playing together as pleasantly as if they had found the happy hunting grounds. The short afternoon waned fast, and the shadows were growing deep when they reached the last part of the game. Ginger had been taken prisoner, and they were tying her to a tree, with her hands bound securely behind her back. She rather enjoyed this part of it, for she intended to show them how brave she could be.

"Now we'll sit around the council fire and decide how to torture her," said Malcolm, when the captive was securely tied. But the fire was out and they had no matches. The lot fell on Malcolm to run up to the house and get some.

"A fire would feel good," said Keith, looking around with a shiver as he seated himself on a log near Ginger. The sun was low in the west, and very little of its light and warmth found its way into the woods where the children were playing.

"It makes me think of Hiawatha," said Ginger, looking down at several long streaks of golden light which lay across the ground at her feet. "Don't you remember how it goes? 'And the long and level sunbeams shot their spears into the forest, breaking through its shield of shadow,' Isn't that pretty? I love Hiawatha. I am going to learn pages and pages of it some day. I know all that part about Minnehaha now,"

"Say it while we are waiting," said Keith, pulling his short trousers down as far as possible, and wishing that he had sleeves, or else that the paint were thicker on his chilly arms.

"All right," began Virginia.

"'Oh the long and dreary winter!
Oh the cold and cruel winter!
Ever thicker, thicker, thicker
Froze the ice on lake and river.'"

"Ugh! Don't!" interrupted Keith, with a shiver. "It makes my teeth chatter, talking about such cold things!"

Just then a shout came ringing down the hill, "Oh, Keith! Come here a minute! Quick!"

"What do you wa-ant?" yelled Keith, in return.

"Come up here! Quick! Hurry up!"

"What do you s'pose can be the matter?" exclaimed Keith, scrambling to his feet. "Maybe the bear has got loose and run away."

"Come and untie me first," said Virginia, "and I'll go, too." Keith gave several quick tugs at the many knotted string which bound her, but could not loosen it. Again the call came, impatient and sharp, "Keith! *Oh*, Keith!"

"Oh, I can't loosen it a bit," said Keith. "You'll have to wait till Malcolm comes with his knife. We'll be back in just a minute. I'll go and see what's the matter."

"Be sure that you don't stay!" screamed Ginger, as the scarlet bedroom slippers and green striped legs flashed out of sight through the bushes.

"Back--in--a--minute!" sounded shrilly through the woods.

Keith found Malcolm on the back porch, pounding excitedly on a box which the express-man had left there a few minutes before.

"It's the camera we have been looking for all week," he cried. "Come on and have a look at it."

"Ginger said to hurry back," said Keith.

"Pshaw! It won't take but a minute. I'll pry the box open in a jiffy."

It was harder work than the boys had supposed, to take the tightly nailed lid from its place, and they were so intent on their work they did not realise how quickly the minutes were passing.

"Isn't it a beauty?" exclaimed Malcolm, when it was at last unpacked. "It's lots bigger and finer than the one papa promised. But that's the way he always does. Oh, isn't it a peach!"

"I'll tell you what," said Keith, dancing up and down in his excitement, until he looked like a ridiculous little clown in the faded pink bathing-suit and his stripes of green paint, "let's take each other's pictures while we are dressed this way. We may never look so funny again, and we can go down and take Ginger, too, while she is tied to the tree."

"Can't now," said Malcolm, "it's too dark down there in the woods by this time. See! there is nothing left now of the sun but those red clouds above the place where it went down. I'm afraid it is too dark even for us up here on the hill; but we can try. You do look funny, just like a jumping-jack or a monkey on a stick."

"Surely Ginger won't mind waiting long enough for us to do it," said Keith. "Anyhow we can never dress up this way again, and grandmother will be coming home very soon, so you take mine quick, and I will take yours."

The boys had had some practice before with a cheap little camera, but this required some studying of the printed directions before they could use it. The first time they tried it the plates were put in wrong, and the second time they forgot to remove the cap. There were other things in the box besides the camera: some beautiful pink curlew's wings, a handsomely marked snake skin, and some rare shells that had been picked up on the Gulf coast. Of course the boys had to examine each new treasure as it was discovered. One thing after another delayed them until it was dusk even on the porch where they stood, and in the woods below a deep twilight had fallen.

Every minute that had sped by so rapidly for the boys, seemed an age to the captive Virginia. Her arms ached from the strain of their unusual position. Swarms of gnats flew about, stinging her face, and mosquitoes buzzed teasingly around her ears. She was unable to move a finger to drive them away.

When the boys had been gone fifteen minutes she thought they must have been away hours. At the end of half an hour she was wild with impatience to get loose, but, thinking they might return any minute, she made no sign of her discomfort. She would be as heroic as the bravest brave ever tortured by cruel savages. As long as it was light she kept up her courage, but presently it began to grow dark under the great beech-trees. A frog down by the spring set up a dismal croaking. What if they should not come back, and her grandmother and Aunt Allison should miss the train, and have to stay in the city all night! Then nobody would come to set her free, and she would have to stay in the lonely woods all by herself, tied to a tree, with her hands behind her back.

At that thought she began calling, "Keith! Keith! Malcolm! Oh, Malcolm!" but only an echo came back to her, as it had to the dying Minnehaha,--a far-away echo that mocked her with its teasing cry of "Mal-colm!" Call after call went ringing through the woods, but nobody answered. Nobody came.

There was a rustling through the leaves behind her, as of a snake gliding around the tree. She was not afraid of snakes in the daytime, and when she was unbound, but she shrieked and turned cold at the thought of one wriggling across her feet while she was powerless to get away. Every time a twig snapped, or there was a fluttering in the bushes, she strained her eyes to see what horrible thing might be creeping up toward her. She had no thought that live Indians might be lurking about, but all the terrible stories she had ever heard, of the days of Daniel Boone and the early settlers, came back to haunt the woods with a nameless dread.

She felt that she was standing on the real Kentucky that the Indians meant, when they gave the State its name. "*Dark and bloody ground! Dark and bloody ground*!" something seemed to say just behind her. Then the trees took it up, and all the leaves whispered, "*Sh--sh, sh! Dark and bloody ground! Sh--sh*!"

At that she was so frightened that she began calling again, but the sound of her own voice startled her. "Oh, they are not coming," she thought, with a miserable ache in her throat, that seemed swelling bigger and bigger. "I'll have to stay here in the woods all night. Oh, mamma! mamma!" she moaned, "I am so scared! If you could only come back and get your poor little girl!"

Up to this time she had bravely fought back the tears, but just then a screech-owl flapped down from a branch above her with such a dismal hooting that she gave a nervous start and a cry of terror. "Oh, that frightened me so!" she sobbed. "I don't believe I can stand it to be out here all night alone with so many horrible creepy things everywhere. And nobody cares! Nobody but papa and mamma, and they are away, way off in Cuba. Maybe I'll never see them any more," At that the tears rolled down her face, and she could not move a hand to wipe them away. To be so little and miserable and forsaken, so worn out with waiting and so helpless among all these unknown horrors that the dark woods might hold, was worse torture to the imaginative child than any bodily pain could have been.

It was just as her last bit of courage oozed away, and she began to cry, that the boys suddenly realised how long they had left her.

"It must be as dark as a pocket in the woods by this time," exclaimed Malcolm. "What do you suppose Ginger will say to us for leaving her so long?"

"You will have to take a knife to cut her loose," said Keith. "I tried to untie the knots before I came away, but I couldn't move them."

"My pocket-knife is up-stairs," answered Malcolm. "I'll get something in the dining-room that will do."

He was rushing out again with a carving-knife in his hand, when he came face to face with his grandmother and Aunt Allison. The boys had been so interested in their camera that they had not heard the train whistle, or the sound of footsteps coming up on the front veranda. Pete was lighting the hall lamps as the ladies came in, and he turned his back to hide the broad grin on his face, as he thought of the sight which would soon greet them. Mrs. MacIntyre gave a gasp of astonishment and sank down in the nearest chair as Malcolm came dashing into the bright lamplight.

His turkey feathers were all awry, standing out in a dozen different directions from his head, his blanket trailed behind him, and the fringe was hanging in festoons from his leggins, where it had come unpinned. The red paint on his face made him look as if he had been in a fight with the carving-knife he carried, and had had the skin peeled off his face in patches.

Wild as he looked, his appearance was tame beside that of the impish-looking little savage who skipped in after him, in the scarlet bedroom slippers, pink striped bathing-suit and green striped skin.

"Keith MacIntyre, what have you been doing to yourself?" gasped his grandmother. Both boys began an excited exclamation, but were stopped by Miss Allison's question, "Where is Virginia? Have you two little savages scalped her?"

64

"She's tied to a tree down by the spring," answered Malcolm. "We are just starting down there now to cut her loose. You see we were playing Indian, and she was tied up to be tortured, and we forgot all about her being there--"

But Miss Allison waited to hear no more. "The poor little thing!" she exclaimed. "Tied out there alone in the dark woods! How could you be so cruel? It is enough to frighten her into spasms."

"I'm awfully sorry, Aunt Allison!" began Malcolm, but his aunt was already out of hearing. Out of the door she ran, through the dewy grass and the stubble of the field beyond, regardless of her dainty spring gown, or her new patent leather shoes. Malcolm and Keith dashed out after her, ran on ahead and were at the spring before she had climbed the fence into the woodland.

Virginia was not crying when the boys reached her. She remembered that she had once called Malcolm "Rain-in-the-face" because she caught him crying over something that seemed to her a very little reason, and she did not intend to give him a chance to taunt her in the same way. She was glad that it was too dark for him to notice her tear-swollen eyes.

"Whew! It's dark down here!" said Keith. "Were you frightened, Ginger?" he asked, as he helped Malcolm unfasten the cords that bound her. But Ginger made no reply to either questions or apologies. She walked on in dignified silence, too deeply hurt by their neglect, too full of a sense of the wrong they had done her, to trust herself to speak without crying, and she intended to be game to the last. But when she came upon Miss Allison, and suddenly found herself folded safe in her arms, with pitying kisses and comforting caresses, she clung to her, sobbing as if her heart would break.

"Oh, auntie! It was so awful!" was all she could say, but she repeated it again and again, until Miss Allison, who had never seen her so excited before, was alarmed. The boys, who had run on ahead to the house again, before she gave way to her feelings, were inclined to look upon it all as a good joke, for they had no idea how much she had suffered, and did not like it because she would not speak to them. They changed their minds when Miss Allison came out of Virginia's room a little later, and told them that the fright had given the child a nervous chill, and that she had cried herself to sleep.

"We didn't mean to do it," said Keith, penitently. "We just forgot, and I'm mighty sorry, truly I am, auntie!"

"I am not scolding you," said Miss Allison, "but if I were either of you boys, I wouldn't wear my little white flower when I dressed for dinner to-night. Instead of being the protector of a distressed maiden, as the old knights would have said, you have done her a wrong,--a serious one I am afraid,--and that wrong ought to be made right as far as possible before you are worthy to wear the badge of knighthood again."

"We'll go and beg her pardon right now," said Malcolm.

"No, she is asleep now, and I do not want her to be disturbed. Besides, a mere apology is not enough. You must make some kind of atonement. The first thing for you to do, however, is to get some turpentine and remove that paint. Where did you get it, boys?"

"Out of your paint-box, Aunt Allison," said Malcolm. "We didn't think you would care. I was only going to take a little, but it soaked in so fast that I had to use two tubes of it."

"I used more than that," confessed Keith, looking at her with his big honest eyes; "but I got so interested pretending that I was turning into a real Indian, that I never thought about its being anybody else's paint, Aunt Allison, truly I didn't!"

She turned away to hide a smile. The earnest little face above the striped body was so very comical. Picking up several of the empty tubes that had been squeezed quite flat, she read the labels. "Rose madder and carmine," she said, solemnly, "two of my very most expensive paints."

"Dear me!" sighed Malcolm, "then there's another wrong that's got to be righted. I guess Keith and I weren't cut out for knights. I'm beginning to think that it's a mighty tough business anyhow."

That night, when the boys came down to dinner, no little white flower with its diamond dewdrop centre shone on the lapel of either coat. It had been a work of time to scrub off the paint, and then it took almost as long to get rid of the turpentine, so that dinner was ready long before Keith was finally clad in his flannels. "My throat is sore," he complained to Malcolm at bedtime, but did not mention it to any one else that night. He sat on the side of his bed a moment before undressing, with one foot across his knee, staring thoughtfully at the lamp. Presently, with one shoe in his hand and the other half unlaced, he hopped over to the dressing-table and stood before it, looking at first one picture and then another.

Eight different photographs of his mother were ranged along the table below the wide mirror, some taken in evening dress, some in simple street costume, and each one so beautiful that it would have been hard to decide which one had the greatest charm.

"I wish mamma was here to-night," said Keith, softly, with a little quiver of his lip. "Seems like she's been gone almost always."

He picked up a large Roman locket of beaten silver that lay open on the table. It held two exquisitely painted miniatures on ivory. One was the same sweet face that looked out at him from each of the photographs, the other was his father's. It showed a handsome young fellow with strong, clean-shaven face, with eyes like Keith's, and the same lordly poise of the fine head that Malcolm had.

"Good night, papa, good night, mamma!" whispered Keith, touching his lips hastily to each picture while Malcolm's back was turned. There were tears in his eyes. Somehow he was so miserably homesick.

Next morning, although Keith's throat was not so sore, he was burning with fever by the time his lessons were over. Before his grandmother saw him he was off on his wheel for a long ride, and then, because he was so hot when he came back, he slipped away to the pond with the pink bathing-suit under his coat, and took the swim that he had been looking forward to so long. Nobody knew where he was, and he stayed in the water until his lips and finger-nails were blue. The morning after that he was too ill to get up, and Mrs. MacIntyre sent for a doctor.

"He has always been so perfectly well, and seemed to have such a strong constitution, that I cannot allow myself to believe this will be anything serious," said Mrs. MacIntyre, but at the end of the third day he was so much worse that she sent to the city for a trained nurse, and telegraphed for his father and mother.

They had already left Florida, and were yachting up the Atlantic coast on their way home when the message reached them.

CHAPTER VIII.

"FAIRCHANCE."

Malcolm did his best to atone to Virginia for what she had suffered from the forgetfulness of the two little Indians, but poor Keith was too ill to remember anything about it. He did not know his father and mother when they came, and tossed restlessly about, talking wildly of things they could not understand. It was the first time he had ever been so ill, and as they watched him lying there day after day, burning with fever, and growing white and thin, a great fear came upon them that he would never be any better.

No one put that fear into words, but little by little it crept from heart to heart like a wintry fog, until the whole house felt its chill. The sweet spring sounds and odours came rushing in at every window from the sunny world outside, but it might as well have been mid-winter. No one paid any heed while that little life hung in the balance. The servants went through the house on tiptoe. Malcolm and Virginia haunted the halls to discover from the grave faces of the older people what they were afraid to ask, and Mrs. MacIntyre was kept busy answering the inquiries of the neighbours. Scarcely an hour passed that some one did not come to ask about Keith, to leave flowers, or to proffer kindly services. Everybody who knew the little fellow loved him. His bright smile and winning manner had made him a host of friends.

There was no lack of attention. His father and mother, Miss Allison, and the nurse watched every breath, every pulse-beat; and a dozen times in the night his grandmother stole to the door to look anxiously at the wan little face on the pillow.

"It is so strange," said his mother to the nurse one day. "He keeps talking about a white flower. He says that he can't right the wrong unless he wears it, and that Jonesy will have to be shut up and never find his brother again. What do you suppose he means?"

The nurse shook her head. She did not know. Just then Mrs. MacIntyre heard her name called softly, "Elise," and her husband beckoned her to come out into the hall. "I want to show you something in Allison's room," he said, leading her down the hall to his sister's apartment. On each side of the low writing-desk stood a large photograph, one of Malcolm in his suit of mail, the other of Keith in the costume of jewel-embroidered velvet, like the little Duke of Gloster's.

"Oh, Sydney! How beautiful!" she exclaimed, as she swept across the room and knelt down before the desk for a better view. Leaning her arms on the desk, she looked into Keith's pictured face with hungry eyes. "Isn't he lovely?" she repeated. "Oh, he'll never look like that again! I know it! I know it!" she sobbed, remembering how white was the little face on the pillow that she had just left.

Mr. MacIntyre bent over her, his own handsome face white and haggard. He looked ill himself, from the constant watching and anxiety. "I'd give anything in the world that I own! Everything!" he groaned. "I'd do anything, sacrifice anything, to see him as well and sturdy as he looks there!"

Then he caught up the picture. "What's this written underneath?" he asked, "It is in Keith's own handwriting: '*Live pure speak truth, right the wrong, follow the king. Else wherefore born?*'

"What does it mean, Allison?" he asked, turning to his sister, who was resting on a couch by the window. "It is written under Malcolm's picture, too."

"The dear little Sir Galahads," she said, "I sent for you to tell you about them. The boys intended the pictures as a surprise for you and Elise, so we never sent them. They wanted to tell you themselves about the Benefit and the little waif they gave it for."

She took a little pin from a jewel-case under the sofa pillows, and reaching over, dropped it in her brother's hand. It was a tiny flower of white enamel, with a diamond dewdrop in the centre.

"You may have noticed Malcolm wearing one like it," she said, and then she told them the story of Jonesy and the bear and all that their coming had led to: the Benefit, the new order of knighthood, and the awakening of the boys to a noble purpose.

"The boys fully expect you to stand by them in all this, Sydney," she said, in conclusion, "and play fairy godfather for Jonesy henceforth and for ever. One night, when Keith came up to confess some mischief he had been into during the day, he said:

"'Aunt Allison, this wearing the white flower of a blameless life isn't as easy as it is cracked up to be; but having this little pin helps a lot. I just put my hand on that like the real knights used to do on their sword-hilts, and repeat my motto. It will be easier when papa comes home. Since I've known Jonesy, and heard him tell about the hard times some people have that he knows, it seems to me there's an awful lot of wrong in the world for somebody to set right. Some nights I can hardly go to sleep for thinking about it, and wishing that I were grown up so that I could begin to do my part. I wish papa could be here now. He'd make a splendid knight; he is so big and good and handsome. I don't s'pose King Arthur himself was any better or braver than my father is.'"

A tear splashed down from the mother's eyes as she listened, and, falling on the tiny white flower as it lay in her husband's hand, glistened beside the dewdrop centre like another diamond.

"Oh, Sydney!" she exclaimed, in a heart-broken way. Something very like a sob shook the man's broad shoulders, and, turning abruptly, he strode out of the room.

Down in the dim, green library, where the blinds had been drawn to keep it cool, he threw himself into a chair beside the table. Propping Keith's picture up in front of him against a pile of books, he leaned forward, gazing at it earnestly. He had never realised before how much he loved the little son, who hour by hour seemed slowly slipping farther away from him. The pictured face looked full into his as if it would speak. It wore the same sweet, trustful expression that had shone there the night he talked to Jonesy of the Hall of the Shields; the same childish purity that had moved the old professor to lay his hands upon his head and call him Galahad.

All that gentle birth, college breeding, wealth, and travel could give a man, were Sydney MacIntyre's, and yet, measuring himself by Keith's standard of knighthood, he felt himself sadly lacking. He had given liberally to charities hundreds of dollars, because it was often easier for him to write out a check than to listen to somebody's tale of suffering. But aside from that he had left the old world to wag on as best it could, with its grievous load of wrong and sorrow.

A man is not apt to trouble himself as to how it wags for those outside his circle of friends, when the generations before him have spent their time laying up a fortune for him to enjoy. But this man was beginning to trouble himself about it now, as he paced restlessly up and down the room. He was not thinking now about the things that usually occupied him, his social duties, his home or club, or yacht or horses or kennels. He was not planning some new pleasure for his friends or family, he was wondering what he could do to be worthy of the exalted regard in which he was held by his little sons. What wrong could he set right, to prove himself really as noble as they thought him? He was their ideal of all that was generous and manly, and yet--

"What have I ever done," he asked himself, "to make them think so? If I were to be taken out of the world to-morrow, I would be leaving it exactly as I found it. Who could point to my coffin and say, 'Laws are better, politics are purer, or times are not so hard for the masses now, because this one man willed to lift up his fellows as far as the might of one strong life can reach?' But they will say that of Malcolm, and Keith, if he lives--ah, if he lives!"

An hour later the door opened, and Malcolm came in, softly. "Keith is asking for you, papa," he said, with a timid glance into his father's haggard face. Then he came nearer, and slipped his hand into the man's strong fingers, and together they went up the stairs to answer the summons.

"Did you want me, Keith?"

The head did not turn on the pillow. The languid eyes opened only half-way, but there was recognition in them now, and one little hand was raised to lay itself lovingly against his father's cheek.

"What is it, son?"

The weak little voice tried to answer, but the words came only in gasps. "Brother knows--about Jonesy--keep him from being a tramp! Please let me, papa--do that much good--in my life 'else wherefore--born?'"

"What is it, Keith?" asked his father, bending over him. "Papa doesn't exactly understand. But you can have anything you want, my boy. Anything! I'll do whatever you ask."

"Malcolm knows," was the answer. Then the voice seemed somewhat stronger for an instant, and a faint smile touched Keith's lips. "Give my half of the bear to Ginger. Now--may I have--my--white--flower?"

Throwing back his coat, his father unpinned the little badge from his vest, where he had fastened it for safe-keeping a short time before in the library. A pleased expression flitted over the child's face, as he saw where it had been resting, and when it was fastened in the front of his little embroidered nightshirt, his hand closed over the pin as if it were something very precious, and he were afraid of losing it again.

"Wearing the white flower," they heard him whisper, and then the little knight slept.

It was hours afterward when he roused again,--hours when the faintest noise had not been allowed in the house; when the servants had been sent to the cottage, and Unc' Henry stationed at the front gate; that no one might drive up the avenue.

Virginia, in a hammock on the veranda, scarcely dared draw a deep breath till she heard the doctor coming down the stairs, just before dark. Then she knew by his face that prayers and skill and tender nursing had not been in vain, and that Keith would live.

So much can happen in a week. In the seven days that followed Keith gradually grew strong enough to be propped up in bed a little while at a time; Captain Dudley and his wife came home from Cuba, and Mr. MacIntyre began to carry out the promise he had made to Keith that day when they feared most he could not live.

The whole Valley rejoiced in the first and second happenings, and were too much occupied in them to notice the third. Carriages rolled in and out of the great entrance gate all day long, for Mrs. Dudley had always been a favourite with the old neighbours, and they gave a warm welcome to her and her gallant husband. Virginia followed her father and mother about like a loving shadow, and Keith was so interested in the wonderful stories they told of their Cuban experiences that he never noticed how much his father and Malcolm were away from home. Sometimes they would be gone all day together, consulting with the old professor, overseeing carpenters, or making hasty trips to the city. Jonesy's home, that had been so long only a beautiful air-castle, was rapidly taking shape in wood and stone, and the painters would soon be at work on it.

Mr. MacIntyre had never been more surprised than he was when Malcolm unfolded their plan to him. It did not seem possible that two children could have thought of it all, and arranged every detail without the help of some older head.

"It just grew," said Malcolm, in explanation. "First Keith said how lovely it would have been if we had made enough money at the Benefit to have bought a home for Jonesy in the country, where he could have a fair chance to grow up a good man. Just a comfortable little cottage with a garden, where he could be out-of-doors all the time, instead of in the dirty city streets; then nobody could call him a 'child of the slums' any more. Then we said it would be better if there were some fields back of the garden, so that he could learn to be a farmer when he was older, and have some way to make a living. We talked about it every night when we went to bed, and kept putting a little more and a little more to it, until it was as real to us as if we had truly seen such a place. There were vines on the porches, and a big Newfoundland dog on the front steps, and a cow and calf in the pasture, and a gentle old horse that could plough and that Jonesy could ride to water.

"We told Ginger, and she thought of a lot more things; some little speckled pigs in a pen and kittens in the hay-mow, and ducks on the pond, and an orchard, and roses in the yard. She said we ought to call the place 'Fairchance,' because that's what it would mean for Jonesy and Barney (you know we would send for Barney first thing we did, of course), and it was Ginger who first thought of getting some nice man and his wife to take care of the boys. She said there are plenty of people who would be glad to do it, just for the sake of having such a good home. Ginger said if we could do all that, and keep Jonesy and his brother from growing up to be tramps like the man we bought the bear from, it would be serving our country just as much as if we went to war and fought for it. Ginger is a crank about being a patriot. You ought to hear her talk about it. And Aunt Allison said that 'an ounce of prevention is worth a pound of cure,' and that to build such a place as our 'Fairchance' would be a deed worthy of any true knight."

"How are you expecting to bring this wonderful thing to pass?" asked his father, as Malcolm stopped to take breath. "Do you expect to wave a wand and see it spring up out of the earth?"

"Of course not, papa!" said Malcolm, a little provoked by his father's teasing smile. "We were going to ask you to let us take the money that grandfather left us in his will. We won't need it when we are grown, for we can earn plenty ourselves then, and it seems too bad to have it laid away doing nobody any good, when we need it so much now to right this wrong of Jonesy's."

"But it is not laid away," answered Mr. MacIntyre. "It is invested in such a way that it is earning you more money every year; and more than that, it was left in trust for you, so that it cannot be touched until you are twenty-one."

"Oh, papa!" cried Malcolm, bitterly disappointed. He had hard work to keep back the tears for a moment; then a happy thought made his face brighten. "You could lend us the money, and we would pay you back when we are of age. You know you promised Keith you would do anything he wanted, and that is what he was trying to ask for?"

Mr. MacIntyre put his arm around the earnest little fellow, and drew him to his knee, smiling down into the upturned face that waited eagerly for his answer.

"I only asked that to hear what you would say, my son," was the answer. "You need have no worry about the money. I'll keep my promise to Keith, and Jonesy shall have his home. I'm not a knight, but I'm proud to be the father of two such valiant champions. Please God, you'll not be alone in your battles after this, to right the world's wrongs. I'll be your faithful squire, or, as we'd say in these days, a sort of silent partner in the enterprise."

Several days after this a deed was recorded in the county court-house, conveying a large piece of property from old Colonel Lloyd to Malcolm and Keith MacIntyre. It was the place adjoining "The Locusts," on which stood a fine old homestead that had been vacant for several years. The day after its purchase a force of carpenters and painters were set to work, and two coloured men began clearing out the tangle of bushes in the long-neglected garden.

Jonesy knew nothing of what was going on, and wondered at the long conversations which took place between the old professor and Mr. MacIntyre, always in German. It was the professor who found some one to take care of the home, as Virginia had suggested. He recommended a countryman of his, Carl Sudsberger, who had long been a teacher like himself. He was a gentle old soul who loved children and understood them, and a more motherly creature than his wife could not well be imagined. Everything throve under her thrifty management, and she had no patience with laziness or waste. Any boy in whose bringing up she had a hand would be able to make his way in the world when the time came for it.

Mrs. Dudley and Miss Allison helped choose the furnishings, but Virginia felt that the pleasure of it was all hers, for she was taken to the city every time they went, and allowed a voice in everything. Several trips were necessary before the house was complete, but by the last week in May it was ready from attic to cellar.

It was the "Fairchance" that the boys had planned so long, with its rose-bordered paths, the orchard and garden and outlying fields. Nothing had been forgotten, from the big Newfoundland dog on the doorstep, to the ducks on the pond, and the little speckled pigs in the pen. The day that Keith was able to walk down-stairs for the first time, Mr. MacIntyre went to Chicago, taking Jonesy with him, to find Barney and bring him back. He was gone several days, and when he returned there were three boys with him instead of two: Jonesy, Barney, and a little fellow about five years old, still in dresses.

Malcolm met them at the train, and eyed the small newcomer with curiosity. "It is a little chap that Barney had taken under his wing," explained Mr. MacIntyre. "Its mother was dead, and I found it was entirely dependent on Barney for support. They slept together in the same cellar, and shared whatever he happened to earn, just as Jonesy did. I hadn't the heart to leave him behind, although I didn't relish the idea of travelling with such a kindergarten. Would you believe it, Dodds (that's the little fellow's name) *never saw a tree in his life* until yesterday? He had never been out of the slums where he was born, not even to the avenues of the city where he could have seen them. It was too far for him to walk alone, and street-cars were out of the question for him,--as much out of reach of his empty pockets as the moon."

"Never saw a tree!" echoed Malcolm, with a thrill of horror in his voice that a life could be so bare in its knowledge of beauty. "Oh, papa, how much 'Fairchance' will mean to him, then! Oh, I'm so glad, and Keith--why, Keith will want to stand on his head!"

They drove directly to the new place. It was late in the afternoon, and the sunshine threw long, waving shadows across the yard. Mrs. Sudsberger sat on the front porch knitting. A warm breeze blowing in from the garden stirred the white window curtains behind her with soft flutterings. The coloured woman in the kitchen was singing as she moved around preparing supper, and her voice floated cheerily around the corner of the house:

"Swing low, sweet chariot, comin' fer to carry me home,
 Swing low, sweet char-i-*ot*, comin' fer to carry me home!"

A Jersey cow lowed at the pasture bars, and from away over in the woodland came the cooing of a dove. Three little waifs had found a home.

Mr. MacIntyre looked from the commonplace countenances of the boys climbing out of the carriage to Malcolm's noble face. "It is a doubtful experiment," he said to himself. "They may never amount to anything, but at least they shall have a chance to see what clean, honest, country living can do for them." And then there swept across his heart, with a warm, generous rush, the impulse to do as much for every other unfortunate child he could reach, whose only heritage is the poverty and crime of city slums. He had seen so much in that one short visit. The misery of it haunted him, and it was with a happiness as boyish and keen as Malcolm's that he led these children he had rescued into the home that was to be theirs henceforth.

Keith did not see "Fairchance" until Memorial Day. Then they took him over in the carriage in the afternoon, and showed him every nook and corner of the place. There were six boys there now, for room had been made for two little fellows from Louisville, whom Mr. MacIntyre had found at the Newsboys' Home. "I've no doubt but that there'll always be more coming," he said to Mr. Sudsberger, with a smile, as he led them in. "When you once let a little water trickle through the dyke, the whole sea is apt to come pouring in."

"Happy the heart that is swept with such high tides," answered the old German. "It is left the richer by such floods."

Several families in the Valley were invited to come late in the afternoon to a flag-raising. The great silk flag was Virginia's gift, and Captain Dudley made the presentation speech. He wore his uniform in honour of the occasion. This was a part of what he said:

"This Memorial Day, throughout this wide-spread land of ours, over every mound that marks a soldier's dust, some hand is stretched to drop a flower in tender tribute. Over her heroic dead a grateful country wreathes the red of her roses, the white of her lilies, and the blue of her forget-me-nots, repeating even in the sweet syllables of the flowers the symbol of her patriotism,--the red, white, and blue of her war-stained banner.

"My friends, I have followed the old flag into more than one battle. I have seen men charge after it through blinding smoke and hail of bullets, and I have seen them die for it. No one feels more deeply than I what a glorious thing it is to die for one's country, but I want to say to these little lads looking up at this great flag fluttering over us, that it is not half so noble, half so brave, as to live for it, to give yourselves in untiring, every-day living to your country's good. To 'let *all* the ends thou aim'st at be thy country's, thy God's, and truth's.' I would rather have that said of me, that I did that, than to be the greatest general of my day. I would rather be the founder of homes like this one than to manoeuvre successfully the greatest battles.

"May the 'Two Little Knights of Kentucky' go on, out through the land, carrying their motto with them, until the last wrong is righted, and wherever the old flag floats a 'fair chance' may be found for every one that lives beneath it. And may these Stars and Stripes, as they rise and fall on the winds of this peaceful valley, whisper continuously that same motto, until its lessons of truth and purity and unselfish service have been blazoned on the hearts of every boy who calls this home. May it help to make him a true knight in his country's cause."

There was music after that, and then old Colonel Lloyd made a speech, and Virginia and the Little Colonel gathered roses out of the old garden, so that every one could wear a bunch. A little later they had supper on the lawn, picnic fashion, and then drove home in the cool of the evening, when all the meadows were full of soft flashings from the fairy torches of a million fireflies.

With Keith safely covered up in a hammock, they lingered on the porch long after the stars came out, and the dew lay heavy on the roses. They were building other air-castles now, to be rebuilt some day, as Jonesy's home had been; only these were still larger and better. The older people were planning, too, and all the good that grew out of that quiet evening talk can never be known until that day comes when the King shall read all the names in his Hall of the Shields.

"It has been such a beautiful day," said Virginia, leaning her head happily against her mother's shoulder. Then she started up, suddenly remembering something. "Oh, papa!" she cried, "let's end it as they do at the fort, with the bugle-call. I'll run and get my old bugle, and you play 'taps.'"

A few minutes later the silvery notes went floating out on the warm night air, through all the peaceful valley; over the mounds in the little churchyard, wreathed now with their fresh memorial roses; past "The Locusts" where the Little Colonel lay a-dreaming. Over the woods and fields they floated, until they reached the flag that kept its fluttering vigil over "Fairchance."

Jonesy sat up in bed to listen. Many a reveille would sound before his full awakening to all that the two little knights had made possible for him, but the sweet, dim dream of the future that stole into his grateful little heart was an earnest of what was in store for him. Then the bugle-call, falling through the starlight like a benediction, closed the happy day with its peaceful "Good night."

Made in the USA
Monee, IL
30 April 2022